MATED TO THE CYBORGS

INTERSTELLAR BRIDES® PROGRAM: THE COLONY - 2

GRACE GOODWIN

Published by KSA Publishers
Goodwin, Grace
Mated to the Cyborgs, Interstellar Brides® Program: The Colony - 2

Cover Copyright © 2019 by Grace Goodwin
Images/Photo Credit: Deposit Photos: RomarioIen, Angela_Harburn

GET A FREE BOOK!

INTERSTELLAR BRIDES® PROGRAM

YOUR mate is out there. Take the test today and discover your perfect match. Are you ready for a sexy alien mate (or two)?

1

*K*ristin Webster, Interstellar Brides Processing Center, Earth

WHEN I FELT the press of a cock...*there*, I stilled, my breath catching. My first thought was panic. *How did he know?* I'd never told anyone my secret.

Never.

Wanting him there now, stretching me, filling me—it was wrong. So wrong. Oh, I knew guys wanted anal sex, at least if every porno was to be a guide. And I knew too much about pornos since I'd worked in the human trafficking division of the FBI for three years—but I'd never been asked to try this. Never even been prodded by accident. Not even a *whoops, I missed your pussy and ended up in your ass instead* conversation.

I'd been vanilla in bed, never admitting to anyone what I really wanted or needed. Always afraid. Until now.

Now, I felt that cock pressing against my back entrance

and *wanted* it to open me up and slip inside. Slide deep and fuck me. Stretch me. Make me burn a little. His cock was bigger than anything I'd ever played with, bigger than I'd imagined. And it was slipping just inside me. *There.* Against all reason, all sanity, I wanted him to hurry. To go deep and fill me up, stretch me open until I begged for mercy, sure nothing else would fit. To fuck me the way I'd been too afraid to admit to any other man. Ever.

Why?

Because there was a huge cock stretching my pussy already—but one cock wasn't enough. Not for me. Not for naughty, naughty Kristin.

I was a bad girl. And no one knew. No one suspected. But, God, I wanted to be a bad, bad girl...I wanted him to pull my hair and make me beg, bite me until it hurt and pinch my nipples until they burned. And every single one of those desires was buried so deep inside me that I'd never spoken them aloud. Not once. Not even to myself.

But dream me didn't care. She lusted. Ached. Was completely at ease between the two powerful male bodies. She didn't worry about asking for what she wanted. Admitting she needed *more* than the standard wham-bam, missionary position nightmare that most people settled for in life. Somewhere, deep inside, she *knew* they'd take care of her. Give her everything. Make her scream and come and beg for more.

I wanted to beg like that. To trust. To let go. Surrender.

This was a dream. It had to be. I'd never had a real threesome. Not straight laced, FBI agent Kristin Webster. Men were afraid of me, or thought I was too hard, too cold, too jaded by what I'd seen in the field ever to want to be dominated in bed.

They were wrong. So, wrong.

But this didn't *feel* like a dream. No, it felt real. The *cocks* felt real. The hot skin of the man beneath me—I was riding him like a Wyoming cowgirl—his thick cock filling my pussy so completely, rubbing against places inside me that had come alive for the first time. Was that my G-spot he was hitting?

I whimpered when that flared head nudged it, again and again.

My clit rubbed against him every time he thrust up into me. Deep, so deep that he bottomed out. I arched my back, shifting so I could take as much of him as possible. More, even. My hands pressed against silky sheets by his shoulders, cool against my heated skin and I arched my back, offering myself to the man behind me where he played. By body begged, saying what I could not speak as I spread me knees wider and clenched my muscles, hoping to draw his attention.

We were all slippery, and I knew it was some kind of oil that made us slick, the aroma rich and exotic. Heady. The smell blended with sex and skin and man. My men. Their unique scents familiar to me, to this body, and they filled my head with lust, and memories of other encounters, orgasms. Pleasure. They drowned me in pleasure.

Big hands were on my hips, guiding me, moving me at the whim of the man beneath me. A second set of hands reached around from behind to cup and play with my nipples. They were hard points, so sensitive I clenched and squeezed my inner walls with every hard pull. Since when had my nipples been tied directly to my pussy?

With one delicious twist, I moaned.

"I'm going to come," I cried, and I didn't recognize my

voice. Who was that wild woman? I couldn't play with my clit even if I wanted to because I didn't have permission, and that made me hotter. More desperate. I knew my mates wouldn't let me. Knew my orgasms belonged to them. How I knew this, I had no idea. It was a dream. A strange, hot, incredible dream.

I wasn't going anywhere and I didn't want to. I wanted them to finish what they started. I wanted them to break me open and take everything, every last ounce of pleasure and control. I wanted to belong to them, completely. No holding back. No freaking rules. Just me...and them.

Mine. They were *mine*.

The ferocity of the thought had me sinking down onto my mate's cock and wiggling, riding him with my clit, reaching for what I needed. I was mindless now. I needed to come. I needed them to let me come.

A hand came down on my right ass cheek, the sound of it a loud crack in the room. It only made me clench down on the cock fucking me and pushed me even closer to release.

"No coming, mate." His hot hand landed on my ass again, the sharp sound like a drug to my overloaded senses. "Not until I'm in your ass and we are claiming you together," the man behind me said. "You'll come harder. It will be so much better."

I shook my head, lost. I didn't want to wait. I needed him now.

He spanked me again. A gasp escaped my lips. It stung, but then quickly morphed into heat, bright and sharp in my mind. I grinned as my body shuddered, the effect of his touch perhaps the opposite of what he intended.

"If you keep doing that, I'm going to come," I said, licking my dry lips.

I heard the rough rumble of men's laughter.

"Our naughty female." The words were said with praise as the cock pressed harder against my back entrance, the coating of oil making it slide inside me smoothly, easily.

I expected to feel pain—didn't a cock that big hurt?— but I didn't. I only groaned at the silent pop as the head of his cock slipped past the tight ring of muscle that had tried to keep him out.

Stuffed, filled, I'd never felt anything like this. I collapsed on top of my mate's chest, content to let them take me, fuck me, love me. *Nothing* was going to keep these two from claiming me. I had no intention of stopping them. It felt so, so good.

They moved and I cried out, the feel of having two cocks moving inside me was too much for me to fight. I couldn't hold back. I was so filled.

My orgasm built and my pussy fluttered with the beginning of a spasm, but the man behind me groaned and both of them stopped moving.

"No. Not yet. Not without permission." Both of them remained still as my body came back from the edge and my awareness of the men, my body, the room slowly returned to me. I could hear their ragged breaths, feel the tightening of their grips on me, the slick slide of their cocks in me. I could feel *everything* and it was coalescing into this perfect, bright, hot ball that was going to burst.

"Please, please move. Please," I begged, trying to shift my hips, rub my clit against the one beneath me. Anything.

"Not yet, mate."

I was beyond all reason now. Every nerve ending in my body was awake, my skin tingling, my body so sensitive that I had to fight to remember words, to force my lips to form around the sounds so I could beg. "Please, I can't wait."

"Then we will say the words now."

"Do *something,*" I whimpered. Tears slipped down my cheeks, the only release I was offered in this moment suspended between them, conquered. Owned.

"Do you accept my claim, mate?" The man beneath me spoke, his voice smooth and deep. Clear and even, considering we were fucking and his cock was hard as granite inside my pussy. "Do you give yourself to me and my second freely, or do you wish to choose another Primary Male?"

"Yes," I cried, my breathing ragged as I adjusted to having two big cocks in me. I knew that wasn't the word he wanted, what I was supposed to say, but my pussy spasmed again and I couldn't say more. Couldn't focus on talking.

"Say the words, mate, then we'll move. We'll fuck you just as you want."

I licked my dry lips. If I wanted them to take me, give me what I needed, I had to focus, as least for a few seconds.

This was important. The claiming. Somehow, dream me knew this mattered. As in, forever, sacred vows. Thankfully, she knew what to say. "I accept your claim, warriors."

My vow spoken, my mates growled, their control pushed to its limit. I realized then I wasn't the only one barely hanging on.

"Then we claim you in the rite of naming. You belong to us and we shall kill any other warrior who dares to touch you."

"May the gods witness and protect you." A chorus of voices sounded around us.

We weren't alone?

Oh, my god. And those voices? They were deep. Male. And there were a lot of them.

My inner walls clenched as I discovered we were being watched. I had one cock in my pussy and one in my ass, I was naked and begging, and we were being *watched*?

Part of me, the conservative, uptight, never-break-the-rules part of me was screaming in my head. But dream me didn't care. It was too much. Another first for me—I'd never imagined exhibitionism to be hot—and I loved knowing others were watching, wanting, devouring our lust with their eyes, yet forbidden to touch.

If I'd known I was such a dirty girl, I'd have sought out two men who could give it to me before now.

A hand came down on my ass as both cocks pulled out, then slid deep, filling me completely together, their thrusts hard and fast as I cried out at the pleasure and pain of being taken so completely.

"No other will give this to you," the one behind me growled, his hand fisting in my hair to pull my head back. He angled my head up until I looked at him over my shoulder and kissed me hard and deep as the man below took over playing with my nipples. Had I said the last out loud?

His tongue thrust deep as his cock moved inside my ass, hard and fast and without mercy. The scream built in my throat as my body tightened around them both, the pain of holding back building like a bomb about to explode inside me.

He broke the kiss and bit down gently on my ear. "Come, mate. Now."

At his dominating tone, the morphing heat from that

smack to my ass and the cocks buried deep inside me, I shattered.

I screamed and bucked as they held me locked between them. My muscles tightened then went limp, tightened again, giving over to the pleasure they were giving me. My palms pressed into the hot skin of the man's chest below me, my fingers curling and most likely leaving small welts as my pussy tightened on him like a fist.

The men moved faster, unrelenting, fucking me and alternating their motions, keeping the feelings of bliss alive, making my pleasure linger and linger until I had no breath left and I exploded again, the sharp tug of my mate's hand in my hair holding me in place like iron shackles, my only physical anchor. I could not pull free, could not escape their possession, could do nothing but accept the dominant thrusts of their cocks as they claimed me with a hunger that drove my own. I spiraled again, so close, my body not yet satisfied, and whimpered a denial as I felt them stiffen and swell, fill me to the brink, then come.

Their seed spurted hotly into me, so much so that it seeped out, coated me. Them. We were one, united, and I'd been the one to do it, to create this family. They were mine.

The mate at my back licked my neck, tasting the glistening moisture their attentions had wrung from me. "Good girl, showing everyone how your mates bring you pleasure. There is no question that you belong to us. You want us, need us, just as much as we need you."

I felt the man before me sit up, strong and powerful muscles rippling beneath my palms. His mouth crushed my lips in a searing kiss as I felt the man behind me nibble my ear, my neck, gently bite down on my shoulder. The pain made my hips jerk and I slid down, drove both of their cocks deeper inside me as I surrendered completely, trapped between them. Worshipped by both.

"Mate," they repeated, over and over. Neither pulled out. Neither softened within me. I knew we weren't done. We'd fuck again and all I could say was...

"Please." I needed them to hurry. To move. To bite me. Spank me. Fuck me like they'd never get enough. I was still on the edge, my appetite for them nowhere near appeased. "Please, hurry."

"Miss Webster."

That voice was annoying, and didn't belong to my mates. I ignored it, focusing on the heated bodies surrounding me. I needed more. Why weren't they moving? Talking? Fucking me? Making me theirs. Making me *feel*.

"Please," I begged again. "Give it to me. Both of you."

"Miss Webster!"

It wasn't a man's voice who was talking now, but a woman's, and her voice was loud and full of intensity that had nothing to do with sex. Or orgasms. Or hard, thrusting cocks.

No. No. No. I fought to hold on to them, to the pleasure, but my mates faded, like I was truly waking up from a dream. One hot, fucking amazing dream.

I opened my eyes, blinked. Then again.

Crisp white walls. A less-than-appealing hospital gown rubbing my sensitive nipples. Arms strapped to my sides, restraining me, as I sat in a chair with weirdo computer gadgets and sensors attached to my body and head. I was naked under the gown, the hard seat beneath my bottom smeared and wet with my arousal.

Warden Egara, with her dark hair, kind eyes and stern expression staring at me like I was a freak in the circus.

Oh. My. God.

Embarrassing. God, could she smell it? Did I smell like sex? What would she think of me? Was I supposed to be this turned on? I doubted it. I must be some kind of mutant show for her today. Poor little Kristin, who couldn't trust men. Who hadn't had a date in three years. Who saw a man on his phone and assumed he was watching child pornography, or hiring hookers, or dozens of other things I'd seen wicked men do.

There was a reason I was here, at the Interstellar Brides processing center. I'd seen too much. I needed a fresh start. And maybe I could turn off my brain and actually enjoy myself in bed with an alien, a guy I knew was honorable and who was matched to me by the most advanced dating system ever created. The matching protocols made human website dating look like stone-age tools next to a rocket ship.

I sighed, and blinked at the warden. So, I wasn't having an amazing, sexy threesome with two well-endowed men in a room full of observers. No, I was at the Interstellar Brides testing center. I was strapped into the testing chair and I'd just begged Warden Egara to *give it to me*.

"Can you please just transport me now so I never have to see you again?" I asked. With my wrists restrained to the arms of the very uncomfortable dentist-like chair, I couldn't even cover my face.

In fact, I barely had my butt covered with the stupid hospital gown being open in the back as it was. I wiggled my hips. While my pussy was still heavy and swollen from my arousal and orgasm, I would swear I could still feel the size of the men's cock stretching me wide in both...places.

But my mind was at war with what my body was feeling.

There were no cocks. No hot men pulling my hair, pumping into me and making me come on command.

Instead, the female warden was petite, with dark hair pulled up off her neck in an official bun. Her red uniform had the insignia of the Brides Program on the chest and she had a look of a woman who was kind, but also on the job.

"I assure you, I've heard worse."

I widened my eyes. "I can only imagine what other women have said."

She turned away and moved to sit at the table before me, swiped at her tablet. For a minute, she was quiet, then she looked up at me, smiled. "From your words, it seems that you had two males in your dream. I can tell by your blush that's the case."

I didn't say anything. I just wanted to crawl into a hole and die, or transport off planet.

"You've been matched to a warrior from Prillon Prime. Congratulations."

"You seem very excited about this," I replied. My palms were damp and I had nowhere to wipe them.

"I know firsthand that Prillon males are very virile. Possessive. Dominant."

Yes, that summed up the guys in my dream, and I hadn't even remembered their faces. Only their cocks.

"Firsthand? You were mated?" I asked.

The excitement diminished on her face. "Yes, but that was a long time ago."

I knew from the program's information that a match was for life, at least after the first thirty-day trial period. That meant that something terrible had to have happened to *both* of her mates for her to be back on Earth.

"Do you accept your match?" she asked next.

Did I want to stay on Earth and find a man? Hell, no. My work hunting sex offenders and traffickers had ruined me for any guy on Earth. What they did to women, and worse, children, had me avoiding all of them. Unfair? Yes. There were good guys out there, but I wasn't wasting my time trying to find them among all the bad apples. Working for the FBI exposed me to the worst criminals and the underbelly of society. I knew I was jaded, untrusting and cold. I'd had to build a wall of ice around my heart to survive. The women and children I'd helped didn't need me to be soft or needy. They needed me to be hard, merciless and vicious, just like the criminals I'd spent the last few years hunting.

And I'd played my part. Now I was broken.

No, I needed a fresh start on a planet where I wouldn't look at every man and assume the worst. Why waste time trying to find a guy who wasn't an asshole when I could get the perfect man—or two—with one efficient, well-proven matching test?

And it seemed I was to have two mates. God, I'd never even thought of the possibility before now. Why would I? I didn't even want one Earth man, let alone two.

"I'm matched to one warrior from Prillon, but I get two mates?"

She cocked her head to the side slightly. "Yes, you are matched to one Prillon warrior, but they always claim a mate with a designated second. The warriors of Prillon Prime are well known to battle the Hive in deep space. They have a high rate of casualties and choose a second to protect their mate and care for any children in case the unthinkable happens."

"In case they are killed in action?"

Her gray eyes were sad. "Yes. They would never leave their family unprotected. All Prillon warriors choose a second, a male they trust and respect. This second warrior will be just as devoted a mate as your first. Legally, according to the laws of Prillon Prime, you will be mated to both."

"Like the dream." I remembered the specific wording that he'd said to me and that I'd used to reply. *Our claim.* Not mine.

"Like the dream. Once you meet your mates, you will have thirty days to accept their claim or tell them you wish to be matched to another."

Accept their claim? Yes, I knew what the claiming was like and I squirmed.

"For the record, do you accept this match?" she asked, her voice becoming even toned and official. "Once you accept the match, you will become an official citizen of Prillon Prime. You will not return to Earth, Kristin."

Did I accept the match? If I said yes, I was going to be transported off Earth and to Prillon Prime, several light years away. This wasn't a trip to Italy.

But wasn't this exactly what I wanted? I'd volunteered for this. I'd put my own butt in the stupid hospital gown and submitted to the testing. I'd loved every minute of that dream. I wanted more. I wanted to feel like that woman, wild and wanton and free.

"Yes." There was no going back now. "Yes, I accept the match."

She nodded once, her fingers swiping busily across her tablet. "To follow protocol, please state your name."

"Kristin Webster."

"Have you ever been, or are you now, married?"

"No."

"Any biological offspring?"

"No."

"I am required to inform you, even though I mentioned it already, that you will have thirty days to accept or reject the mate chosen for you by the Interstellar Brides Program's matching protocols."

I took a deep breath, let it out. No more sex crimes unit. No more bad guys. No more FBI. Hell, no more Earth. Just what I'd wanted.

I took a deep breath, let it out. "I guess I'm going to Prillon Prime. When do I get my men?"

I couldn't help but grin at the idea. It seemed insane. It *was* insane.

She looked down at the tablet again, did some more swiping, glanced up. Smiled brilliantly. "How about right now? Your mate resides on a secondary Prillon planet known as The Colony. You've been matched to a warrior with ninety-eight percent compatibility."

The Colony? Never heard of it, but who cared. Alien was alien. "And the second mate is the other two percent?" I wondered.

She stepped back, laughing at my sarcasm. "You could say that."

With one final swipe of her finger, the wall behind me opened, a blue light coming from beyond. I turned my head, but couldn't see anything but the colored glow.

"Don't panic. When you wake, Kristin Webster, your body will have been prepared for their customs and your mates' requirements. He will be waiting for you." She spoke as if from a script, and that meant I wasn't the only woman who panicked right about now.

Two large metallic arms with gigantic needles on the

ends appeared to be headed for the sides of my face. "Hang on a second. What they hell are those things?"

I tried to wiggle away, but that wasn't working since I was still strapped to the damn chair.

"They will insert the Neuroprocessing Units that will integrate with the language centers of your brain, allowing you to speak and understand any language. Be calm and you'll soon be with your mate."

I held my breath as the needles came closer, then pierced the sides of my temples, just above my ears. I winced, but it wasn't really that painful. Once the robot arms retracted, my seat slid backward and I found myself being lowered in a warm, blue-glowing bath. I exhaled and relaxed, for all my fears seemed to melt away.

"Kristin Webster, you are off to your Prillon warrior. I am not biased, since everyone is matched to the planet perfect for them, but I hold a soft spot for those Prillon males. I know you will be happy, as I once was."

I sighed, closing my eyes. Happy? That was the biggest dream of all.

"Your processing will begin in three...two...one."

Everything went black.

aptain Hunt Treval, The Colony, Base 3, New Arrivals Processing Room

IMPATIENCE CLAWED THROUGH ME, making me twist in my seat. Across the table, our four newest arrivals stared at me with a mixture of rage and despair. They attempted to mask their pain, but the anger? The anger was clear in the tense lines of their bodies, the grim set of their lips, the complete lack of humor in their gazes. They were warriors of the Coalition Fleet, had survived capture and torture at the hands of our enemy, the Hive, and now they were *here*.

No one ever wanted to be here.

The fury was something warriors were all too familiar with. And those sent to The Colony had more reason to rage than most. I knew. We all knew. We were outcasts. Abandoned. Rejected by the people we'd fought to protect after suffering agonizing torture and experimentation at the hands of our enemies. We survived, some of us barely, but we were no longer *wanted*. And that was difficult to accept. Arriving at The Colony was proof of that rejection, just as the changes to our bodies were proof that we would never again be whole.

Anger masked a good many other emotions, but especially pain. As warriors, we were the strongest, toughest fuckers in the universe. We didn't do heartbreak. Most of those who'd come through this room in the last two years— since I'd been put in charge of acclimating new arrivals— would prefer torture to tears. These four, it would seem, were no exception.

"I wish to return to my home planet." The large Atlan Warlord, a giant fighter named Rezz, glared at me from his seat. His dinner-plate-sized hands clenched and unclenched on the arms of his chair and I glanced into the corner of the room where my second, Captain Tyran, stood with both an ion blaster and tranquilizer gun at the ready. I met his dark gaze, just for a moment, a question in my eyes.

Tyran nodded, the movement nearly imperceptible. He was ready to shoot. Not that he would need the weapons, even on a beast. The Hive had enhanced Tyran's bones and every major muscle group in his body. He was strong, stronger than any living creature I'd seen, including an Atlan in full beast mode. When Tyran and I had been captured together, we'd been friends. After what they'd done to us, I knew there was no other I would trust with a mate, and I'd asked him to be my second.

Needing each other's trust in battle was over. Sharing a mate would hopefully be our future and even more important than anything else we'd done.

When the first mate had been assigned to someone on The Colony, a woman from Earth named Rachel, I'd been skeptical. But watching as she'd held one of us as he died in her arms had changed my mind about the Interstellar Brides Program. About having a mate. I'd wanted a female's gentle hands to caress my flesh, to look upon me with something other than fear. Gods, I wanted that badly, but assumed being exiled to The Colony meant that pleasure would never be mine, that I'd never be granted a mate, never share a hot, willing female with Tyran.

But Rachel's arrival changed everything. Eager, I'd been tested the next day, Tyran the day after. And now, we simply waited and tried not to hope. Hope was painful, filling my chest with an emptiness no amount of drinking or work could fill. Every time I saw Rachel—Lady Rone—with her mates, Governor Maxim and Captain Ryston, that hope grew worse.

I'd learned hope was a dangerous thing. Some was required to survive, but too much and disappointment would be cruel. It was a precarious balance I'd lived with since my own arrival on this planet.

But it had been weeks since my testing, since Tyran's. Hundreds of warriors on The Colony had been tested and no new brides had arrived. Those of us trapped here began to give up on being matched once again. Hope waned. Anger was better. And work.

I had three Coalition warriors before me, and one bone-chilling Hunter from Everis, who, even now, sat separated and distant from the others. From the looks in their eyes, they had zero hope and that was why Tyran kept his hand cautiously hovering over his ion pistol as he stood near the door.

The Hunter, Kiel, had been rescued from a separate section of the Hive building, a section reserved for breeding.

He looked harmless enough, his dark hair and pale skin more like a warrior from Earth or Trion. But he was far from human, the Hunter's skills of his people frightening and unexplainable. They were like phantoms who could see into the darkness of space. Nothing and no one could hide from them.

Kiel was our first Hunter, and I wasn't quite sure yet what we were going to do with him.

None but myself and Governor Rone knew the complete contents of these men's files, but I shuddered to think what the proud and deadly Hunter had endured. The Everians were the Fleet's deadliest assassins, spies and trackers. They made up a large portion of the Coalition Fleet's Intelligence Core, and the Hive, when they captured a Hunter, were absolutely merciless. I was shocked the Hunter had survived.

Kiel of Everis must have a will of iron. Unbreakable. Which was helpful in battle, but not here. I needed these men to work as a team, integrate into our society. Gain some hope that, while their old lives were over, new ones could be forged. It was my job, my duty, to make sure they did.

These men needed work, purpose, a place to live and a new group of brothers-in-arms to help them cope with their new lives.

The Colony wasn't a home, not for any of us. Even with the governor's mate here, it wasn't enough. This place was a prison, our last stop, and we all knew it. Someday, with mates and children, it could become a home for all of us. Until then...

"None of us are going home, Warlord." I pointed to my temple, pulled up the sleeve to reveal my left arm and hand and the metallic hue just beneath the surface of the flesh on my exposed arm. I never wore my armor for these meetings, instead opting for a short-sleeved civilian tunic and pants to remind these warriors that I was not fighting them. I was not the enemy. I, too, had battled, been taken prisoner. Tortured. Escaped. Survived. *Lived.*

Rezz's eyes darted to my arm then lingered on the hand-sewn decoration lining the seams, noticed the green mating collar I wore around my neck, and his frown deepened. That lingering stare, and the disdainful snarl on his lip at the sight of my collar, didn't improve my mood. I'd been wearing it for three months, since the day I'd gone through the bride testing protocols. Wearing it to encourage others to be tested, to show them I had *hope* she would come. That I was already hers, wherever in the universe she was. As my hope waned, the presence of the collar became the source of jokes at mealtimes, the others sneering at my optimism. Some even doubted I'd actually been tested.

I didn't care what those fuckers thought. I had that damn hope. I was determined to be stronger than they. I refused to believe this lonely life was my destiny. I refused to take it off. She would come. Someday.

"I will not remain here, a prisoner," Rezz insisted.

"You aren't a prisoner, Warlord." I sighed and leaned back in my chair, prepared for the worst. Twice in the last ten years a beast had arrived and lost control. A fact not lost on myself or any other Colony officer watching the exchange. Tyran was not the only security in the room. Three warriors per new arrival was my preference. Today, we fell well short. Counting Tyran, there were only seven guards—and none of them were Atlan. If Warlord Rezzer lost his temper and went into beast mode, even with Tyran's strength, we'd most likely have to kill the Atlan. An action I would prefer to avoid.

Once, the thought of executing the beast would have sent me into a spiral of anguish and self-hatred. Regret. Frustration and a sense of betrayal. But he wasn't just dealing with being on The Colony, his beast was, too. It was an internal battle of wills and I had yet to know who would win with Warlord Rezzer.

I knew how he felt. Trapped. Escape one prison to arrive at another. I'd been on the other side of this table with Tyran beside me three years ago. And just before that, we'd spent three agonizing days in the hands of the Hive Integration Units before the Coalition ReCon team got us out of there. We'd been lucky. Salvageable. Although it hadn't felt like luck at the time.

Now, the only emotion flowing through me, as I watched Rezz fight for control, was resignation. He would either control himself, or he would not. There was no half-measure.

And he wasn't wrong. Although technically, this wasn't a prison, none of us would go home. Ever. And although the common perception on the Coalition Worlds was that the warriors of The Colony were contaminated with Hive technology and not fit to re-enter society in their home planets, the truth was worse—but easier to accept.

The Coalition Fleet couldn't stop Hive command communications on a broad scale. Every warrior here had imbedded Hive tech that couldn't be removed, not if we wanted to stay alive. We were only safe on The Colony because we were so deep inside Coalition space that the Hive couldn't reach us to fuck with our minds or control us like puppets. There were a few with experimental implants being tested. We were testing a new scanning and interference frequency generator. And Lady Rone, an expert scientist in brain and body chemistry, was helping us test new ways to strengthen our bodies against Hive attack.

But I knew it might not be enough.

The highest levels of command didn't want to alert the civilians on our planets to the fact that we were having trouble stopping the Hive. It was frightening, and could potentially cause panic. We were proof of that failure and we couldn't uncover that political nightmare with our presence on the home worlds.

The Coalition Fleet was barely holding its own, struggling to hinder the Hive expansion into Coalition-controlled space. We were on the brink of losing this damn war.

When Prince Nial became Prime of our planet, he'd inherited the mantle of command over the entire Coalition Fleet. His family had a long history of military command. His cousin, Zane Deston, was a renowned Battleship Commander and top ranking officer in the Coalition Fleet. The Deston family had been fighting for generations. Prillon Prime was the first world to stand up to the Hive and to recruit others, and the Coalition had grown around us. We'd been fighting a long, long time. Centuries. When Prime Nial took power, he'd lifted the ban on Hive-contaminated warriors going home, especially since he was one of them. One of us. That had led to more revelations... had forced the I.C., the Intelligence Core, to come forward with some hard truths.

We couldn't go home. Ever. Not all of us.

Prime Nial was infected with Hive tech himself. But after his ascension to the throne, he'd met with the I.C., and they'd explained things to him, things those of us on The Colony already knew—that there was no way to ensure he could control himself in the face of a Hive command. The technology imbedded in his body still obeyed its master, and would answer when called.

The Prime had been given a special implant by the I.C., a permanent signal inhibitor designed to keep him free of Hive control. But it was experimental. And even with the inhibitors available, most Coalition planets refused to lift their ban on contaminated warriors rejoining their civilian populations.

Contaminated warriors were too big a risk. I didn't disagree. I had to deal with them on a daily basis. Hell, I was one of them. Hoping that those on Prillon Prime would accept me and Tyran as *normal* was too much, even for me.

Prime Nial did his best, but in the end, most of the Prillon warriors on The Colony, myself and Tryan included, decided to stay. We'd all fought to protect our people. Going home like this, even with the experimental tech the I.C. offered, would place our families in danger and make our sacrifices, and the deaths of so many friends and fellow warriors, worthless. None of us wanted to lead the Hive to them, to turn on them and lose control.

So we stayed in a prison of our own design.

And hoped for a reprieve, for a bit of life to enter our lives.

For a mate.

"This feels like a death sentence." Warlord Rezzer growled and I saw the beginning of his transformation to beast in his face as the bones seemed to melt and elongate, then return to normal. "They should have left me in that cave to die."

"I'm sorry." I motioned to the warriors standing at attention along the walls. "We all felt the same way when we arrived." The room was large enough to hold at least fifty fully armored fighters. With eleven, it felt like an empty cave echoing back our isolation. "But it gets easier. And The Colony has begun receiving mates from the Interstellar Brides Program. As soon as you're settled, you can be tested for a match."

"No." The Altan rose, his shoulders increasing in size as he snarled at me.

"Calm your beast, Rezz." The Prillon warrior dispassionately seated in the chair next to him, Captain Marz, was about my size, and, like me, his hair, skin and eyes were golden, a pale hue associated with the colder regions of our home world, Prillon Prime. That was, until the Hive took him. Now his left eye was a strange, shimmering silver, the Hive tech implanted in his skin turned the flesh a pale silver as well. The color surrounded his affected eye, wrapped around his temple and disappeared beneath his hair. It was like looking in a mirror, and a bit unnerving. I had his file open and knew he had more under his uniform, more Hive scars. We all did. Even scars that weren't physical. That was why we were here.

Rezz rotated his head on his neck, making a series of cracking and popping noises in his spine as he sat back down. From the corner of my eye, I watched Tyran settle back against the wall and we all took a deep breath in relief. Fucking Atlans and their beasts were unpredictable bastards. We'd be lost without them on the ground in the war, but they didn't really belong inside, sitting calmly and talking politics. Not when their beasts were on the edge of losing control either from anger or mating fever. With Rezz, I suspected both.

"Captain Marz. I have assigned the four of you to work together in Section 9. Prime Nial has ordered us to increase fortifications around all Colony bases and prepare of expansion." I focused my attention on the Prillon captain. I'd seen this before. Knew exactly what happened to these warriors. They may not have known each other before their capture, but somewhere in the agony, Captain Marz had been the one to take control, to hold them together. To keep them sane. And now, the Warlord and the other Prillon seated across from me, Lieutenant Perro, depended on Marz. He'd become their group leader. Which was good. These guys were going to need all the friends they could get. Friends, and a sense of purpose. "We need more men to help engineer and fortify the walls there."

Captain Marz nodded and we both ignored Warlord Rezzer who was slowly regaining control.

The Hunter, Kiel, watched and waited like the predator I knew he was. He hadn't spoken, not a single word, but I had no doubt he knew the position of every one of my security forces in the room, including what weapons they carried and how attentive they were being to the meeting. He wasn't part of Captain Marz's group, but I needed to change that. Even a lone hunter needed somewhere to belong, a reason to get out of bed in the morning. And he was the only Everian on Base 3. As far as I knew, he was the only Hunter ever to survive Hive capture.

Silent until now, the other Prillon warrior, Lieutenant Perro, crossed his arms over his chest. His arms were bare of Hive implants, the soft brown of his skin uninterrupted. I'd looked at his file as well. His implants were mostly in the neck and spine, a few in his brain tissue. Should the Hive ever break through here, his brain would probably leak out his ears. But for now, his eyes were clear and sharp, a copper that matched his hair. "What, exactly, are we supposed to do for the next sixty or seventy years? Build walls? I'm a pilot, and a damn good one."

Yes, he was. And insubordinate, and a bit wild. Which was probably what had led to his capture...and ultimately his suffering on the Hive Integration Unit's surgical table.

"I am aware of all your qualifications. Every new arrival spends time building. It helps work out some stress and allows you time to get to know the others. This isn't a place where you can go it alone. During your acclimation, you will be processed and considered for other duties as well.

"We do run ships to the other bases, and we need pilots for those. But most transfer of goods or personnel is done using the transport pads. If the doctors clear you for flight, you may be assigned to an air patrol crew that monitors the planet's outer atmosphere. But, as you are new here, you need time to adjust. Time to heal. You may not agree with that, but for now, you have no choice. None of you will be assigned to critical areas until you've been here for several weeks."

Or longer. Especially if the rest of the warriors didn't like or trust one of them. But I didn't say that. To give them some of that damn hope, I added, "After that, everything is open for consideration."

Captain Marz nodded. "Fine. I assume we've all been assigned quarters in the same area as well."

Thank the gods, this was almost over and Marz was going to take it from here. I saw it in his eyes, the need to make sure his men were protected and taken care of. At least one of them understood the changes they had to accept. If one was willing to try, then he could talk the others around better than I ever could.

I liked Marz instantly, and made a mental note to move him through the process quickly. With the recent Hive attack, and the defection of one of our own, a medical officer named Krael, I needed men I could trust. Men who had honor. Not that the others didn't. The other three had stellar records and survived the worst of the Hive. If they adjusted well, acclimated to their new lives, they'd be put into positions of importance. We valued everyone on The Colony, *if* they wanted to give their all.

Still, traitors surfaced. Krael brought a Hive transmitter onto Base 3, the poisonous frequencies led to many taking ill, including our own Governor, and had led to Captain Brooks' death. He'd been a warrior from Earth who'd been carefree and liked to laugh, even considering what the Hive had done to him. He'd been my friend, and I wanted nothing more than to catch the bastard traitor who'd killed him. Who'd destroyed him from the inside.

I turned to the Hunter, Kiel. Perhaps I had a good use of the Hunter's skills after all. "You have been assigned the same duties and region."

"Of course." His voice was even and unperturbed, like talking to a corpse. I *wanted* him to argue with me, to break through that damn cool reserve. He'd never deal with his pain, his new reality, if he kept everything sealed up tight.

I stood and rolled my shoulders, the tension there making my head ache. Again. I'd never suffered from headaches before—before the Hive put their needles and microscopic implants into me. Now, they were a constant plague, a reminder that I'd never be what I was before.

"Very well. This is Phin, a member of my security team." I angled my head toward the guard. "He'll lead you to your quarters and take you on a tour of Base 3. You report for your first work shift in eighteen hours."

Captain Marz stood, Perro, the Atlan and the Hunter following behind as four of my team led the way down the corridors to the private quarters. The men had arrived with nothing, so it wouldn't take long for them to settle and explore the base. We didn't have many Atlans, and Kiel was our first Hunter. They would, no doubt, draw a crowd and many challenges in the challenge pits.

I watched Tyran size up Warlord Rezzer as he passed and knew my second was thinking the same. Tyran was currently the reigning champion in hand-to-hand combat on Base 3. A position I was sure the Atlan Warlord would enjoy taking from him. If the newcomer could prevail. Tyran wouldn't make it easy for him to do so.

I followed the group to the door, stopping next to Tyran as the new arrivals and their heavily armed escort moved on. "He's going to break you, friend. Like a stick."

$\mathcal{H}$unt

TYRAN GRINNED, the bright light of a challenge accepted in his dark brown eyes. He was my opposite in many ways, his darker skin and hair a stark contrast to my own. His love of organized violence understandable, but sometimes he couldn't stop, took things too far. Ever since our capture, he'd never been the same. But then, none of us were. Tyran, more than any warrior I knew, looked forward to the organized fights. "How long do you think I have?"

I considered. The Atlan would hear about the fighting pits by dinner tonight. By tomorrow, he'd want to knock Tyran from his place as champion. "A day. Maybe two."

"Excellent." Tyran put his weapons away and fell into step beside me as I walked down the hall. Our boots should have been loud on the hard floors, but we had learned to move quietly on our feet. Even Tyran, dressed in full combat armor, moved silently as a shadow beside me. In comparison to my second, I was considered the personable one. I had to be with my job. I couldn't have the new arrivals scared on their first day. Tyran had an aura of darkness about him. We'd been friends before our capture, but after? After, Tyran's silence grew and I had no idea how to fill it. All I could do was hope our mate would heal him from the inside out.

Ruthlessness, precision. Tyran had an accuracy to his movements, to his fighting that men tried for decades to achieve. This had a price. An introverted spirit, an intensity that made others afraid. Especially since he was a Prillon warrior. But I would have no other as my second. I would trust no one else to keep my mate safe.

"Did you meet with the governor this morning?" Tyran asked.

"Yes."

"Any word on Krael?"

My blood chilled as I thought of the Prillon warrior who'd betrayed us all. My fists clenched at the thought of his lack of honor. He'd been a traitor for a long time and we hadn't known it. It set us all on edge. While we had rules to follow on The Colony to keep things civilized, the entire population was made up of veterans, former fighters, and we'd all assumed that honor prevailed. We learned the hard way this was not the case and now we watched one another closely, with greater scrutiny, with a sense of suspicion I had grown to hate. It was hard enough keeping the men here sane without this added concern of traitors walking among us.

"No one can find him. And there are no transport

records. He's either still on the planet, or he used a ship to escape."

"The governor put a price on his head."

"It's not enough." I knew all about it. There was an even larger bounty off planet, courtesy of Prince Nial of Prillon Prime. But it wasn't sufficient. If it were, we'd have Krael in custody. No one outside of The Colony knew why we wanted the bastard, but everyone in the universe knew we wanted him *alive*.

Tyran agreed as we made our way toward the center of Base 3. Our home had changed much the last few weeks. Between the Prime's mate, Lady Deston's, visits, the presence of Ryston's mother, who'd relocated to The Colony to live near her son, and Lady Rone's arrival as the first Colony mate, The Colony had begun to come to life. The Governor's mate, in particular, enjoyed the gardens and had insisted that more be done to make them welcoming. Trees and flowers had been transported in from all Coalition planets with seating scattered throughout. Vines grew everywhere unchecked, lending the place a somewhat wild feel. I'd scoffed for a time, but now the quiet solitude of the area, with its new water fountains and domesticated birds, drew me in and brought me some measure of peace.

Seeing things from their home worlds growing and coming to life here was uplifting. The Colony wasn't a dead planet. We were alive. We just had to remember how to *live* again.

As if I'd conjured her, I looked up to find Lady Rone and the governor walking toward us, both of them looking pleased.

"Captain Hunt! Tyran! It's time. Come quickly!" Lady Rone reached for each of our hands, all but dragging us in the opposite direction. She was one of the only people on The Colony we'd allow to lead us around in this manner, despite the fact that she was tiny in comparison to our Prillon size. If we did not wish to move, nothing would force us, except perhaps an Atlan in full beast mode.

"My lady, what are you doing?" I looked to her Primary Male, Governor Maxim and he, too smiled. A look I'd rarely seen, but with more frequency now that he and his second, Ryston, had been matched through the Interstellar Brides Program.

"Your mate has arrived."

"My mate?" I stopped dead in my tracks, stunned, as my heart raced. My matched mate? She was here? Lady Rone still tugged, then gave up, pulling solely on Tyran. "What? Why didn't anyone tell me I'd been matched or that she was due to arrive?" Normally, we knew in advance, at least a few hours. Not that I would complain, but shock made every word from my lips ripe with idiocy.

Tyran ignored me and walked with Lady Rone's hand wrapped around his elbow as he escorted her toward the transport station, all but leaving me behind. He glanced over his shoulder and I saw something in his gaze I hadn't seen in a long, long time. It wasn't just hope.

It was eagerness.

Maxim slapped me on the back, pulling me from my thoughts. "She's not *your* matched mate, Hunt. She's Captain Tyran's." He called ahead to Tyran. "I assume Hunt is your choice of second?"

Tyran looked stunned, as shocked as I felt, but he answered quickly. "Of course." Tyran's confirmation reached me, and my world, while still upended, settled. Things might be different than I'd expected, but we would adapt. I would adapt. I had no choice now.

We had a mate. That was the only thing that mattered now.

CAPTAIN TYRAN ZAKAR, *The Colony, Base 3*

MY MATE. Holy hell. *My* mate. Not Hunt's, as I'd first thought. Yes, I'd been disappointed, hope dying a slow death by starvation when weeks, then months passed and not one new mate arrived on The Colony. We'd gone to the testing center, went through the process, but neither of us came out with a match. That was three months ago. Until now, we'd heard nothing further about it. I knew Hunt had held onto his hope these long weeks. I'd given that up long ago.

All I remembered of the event was an amazing yet vague sex dream and that I'd left with a cock so hard I worried it was going to puncture through my armor. Fortunately, I'd been able to return to my quarters and take myself in hand, ease the discomfort I knew would only truly be lessened by sinking into my mate.

And now, I was going to have one. I wouldn't be a second, but the matched mate, the Primary Male. I tried to suppress my grin, but it was almost impossible. I felt...gods, I felt good. Elated. Thrilled. Something pretty damn close to happy. There was a female out there in the universe that was perfect for me.

I'd assumed with my dark ways, my darker sexual needs,

that there would be no one similarly inclined. What female would want to be bound and fucked? Blindfolded and helped to her knees? To cry out with pleasure because of a little bite of pain? To be dominated and not simply want, but need her mate to take control?

If Hunt had been the matched mate, I knew he would take his time and seduce our mate. I had been prepared to accept that, to give a mate what she needed and not worry about anything else. Mild, not wild. Tame, not tawdry. Sensual, not sultry.

But this female was mine. Mine. Which meant she wanted exactly what I wanted. She must need what I could give her. We would not have been matched otherwise.

My heart stuttered, thinking she'd reject me as soon as she saw my eye, saw what the Hive had done to me. But then, with Lady Rone on my arm at this very moment, her hand wrapped around my elbow and a happy smile on her face, I remembered that love was blind. She never seemed to notice or even care that her two warriors had been contaminated by the Hive. My mate must be the same because the match had been made *after* I was ruined by the Hive. The testing matched me, cyborg parts and all, to a female. That meant she would want me just as I was.

Right?

Right?

Next to me, Lady Rone had a noticeable skip in her step, reminding me of a happy child. I allowed her happiness to wash over me. I wouldn't worry now. I'd enjoy the moment. They were rare. Elusive. Unfamiliar.

"You must be so excited," Lady Rone told me as we walked toward the transport room. "I can't wait to meet her. I wonder where she's from."

No one would use the term *excited* with me. I was the quiet one, the watcher. The brooding asshole in the corner. And yet I'd been the one matched.

I knew Maxim and Hunt followed a few steps behind. What was Hunt thinking? He was now *my* second. We were friends. The same rank. Equals. Yet he was a leader, outspoken and bold, while I was content to remain in the shadows. That didn't mean I was any less fierce. In fact, I was perhaps more ruthless and cunning than Hunt. I blended in, quiet, an attack was unexpected.

And with a female? It had been a long time since I'd had my way, but I knew my nature. I would take over, watch her, analyze the smallest response. A woman was a puzzle I was all too eager to solve. There was nothing I enjoyed more than discerning her secrets so I could give her everything she wanted, everything she needed, even when she didn't know it, or would not admit her needs to herself.

I'd just assumed it would be Hunt matched, that he would be the Primary Male and I would be his second. I'd hoped for a mate of my own, assumed that my darker needs would be tamed or hidden entirely, but I hadn't considered it a possibility that there could be a woman in the universe perfect for me. Not when Maxim said a match had been made.

Only when he'd said she was *mine.*

"Excited? No. I hope to be worthy of the honor," I admitted to Lady Rone. I stopped and she looked up at me in surprise. I didn't speak of my doubts, my worries that Hunt might not be able to accept his new role. For years, he'd been the one in the lead, always shouting orders. I'd obeyed, followed, not because I could not lead on my own, but because he was my brother-in-arms, and I trusted no one else to ensure his safety.

And if any other arrogant bastard had tried to order me around, I'd have killed him as easily as bowed my head.

"I must get my collars. I do not wish for her to be without one."

Understanding filled her eyes and Maxim and Hunt joined us just outside the transport room. "I assumed you would wish to place your collar about her neck right away," the governor said, his voice deep. "I was the same. We don't need to start a war over an unclaimed female, as nearly happened with Rachel."

Lady Rone smacked her mate on the arm, rolled her eyes. "That's not fair. It's not my fault I am the only mate on the entire planet." She looked to me. "I can't wait to have another woman here to help me hold my own with you Neanderthals. And one from Earth is even better." Her words were laced with something akin to glee. Her eagerness was infectious because it hit me like an ion blast that while Lady Rone was excited to meet a new friend, the female about to arrive was mine.

Mine!

"While I would not usually take such liberties as sending someone to enter your private quarters, I knew haste was important," Maxim said. "I sent someone, Captain, for your collars, since Hunt is your chosen second."

I glanced at my friend. His expression was neutral. Blank. "He is my second," I said it aloud. "If he accepts." I would not have anyone doubt it. I was proud he would share my mate, that we would be a family. But I'd never asked. We'd never had this conversation, both of us presuming he would be the one matched.

But Hunt still wore his green mating collar about his neck, had put it there the moment his testing was finished. The bright green color was clearly visible and a declaration to all that he was ready for a mate. As his friend, I knew he wanted a female with a desperation he hid well. Finding a mate was more than crucial for him. Necessary. Many warriors on The Colony had teased him about it, but he was unaffected, stalwart in his desire. He knew she would come, and he'd been correct. But as it turned out, her arrival would not be as he'd expected.

He could, however, choose to wait for a mate of his own. He did not have to accept a role as my second. He could wait and claim his own mate, should she arrive one day. I would not blame him, if that were his choice.

"It's your decision, Hunt. I know you wanted a match of your own. I will not refuse you should you choose to wait. I can choose another second."

"No." Hunt scowled at me, his objection clear. To be my second, he would have to remove his family colors and replace them with mine. If he was my second, he would wear the blue collar of my family. But would he accept this shift in our roles? Would he be willing to see a shared mate marked and claimed in a blue collar instead of green?

We all looked to Hunt, waited.

He reached behind his neck and removed his collar, held it out to me with a nod.

Relieved, I grinned, taking it from him.

"I am his second," Hunt said, conviction in his tone.

"Good. Now that that's settled—" Maxim turned and the door slid open. We entered the small transport room and my heart rate soared as if I were heading to battle. Adrenaline flooded my brain.

"She should arrive anytime now, Governor," the transport officer said. He looked up just long enough to speak, then returned to the control panel in front of him. The door slid open again and a second officer came to me, holding out three collars, two blue as the deepest sky on Prillon Prime, and one, my lady's, black as deep space until she formally accepted my claim, allowed us to fill her body together. Once she was mine, the collar would turn blue and she would be mine forever. The strips of cloth and imbedded neural technology had only held empty promise, until now. While I knew there was no change in them, they felt different. Soon, they would be affixed about our necks— Hunt, myself and our mate—binding us together, sharing our emotions and desires, making us one—forever.

The black and green grid of the transport pad was easily large enough to hold twenty armed warriors, but was empty. We all stared at it, used to sudden arrivals. But a female was different.

Everything was different. And when I felt the hairs on my body rise, the only sign of the energy shift created by a transport, I knew my life would never be the same again.

There was no going back.

And when a small form appeared on the pad, pale and bare, I felt her presence in my very bones, a heaviness, an ache I couldn't explain. *This* was my mate.

4

IT WAS Hunt who recognized the situation a touch differently and quickly stripped off his tunic, dashed up the few steps to the transport pad and covered the sleeping form.

He turned his head and glared at the two officers manning the transport controls, who both quickly averted their gazes.

"Get a blanket immediately," Lady Rone called.

I heard footsteps, but didn't look away from the fragile female. I couldn't. I couldn't even move, not until Hunt called my name.

With long strides, I closed the distance to my mate and knelt down beside her. She looked like she was asleep, but was she—

My fingers went to her pale neck, felt along the soft skin

for her pulse, felt it sure and strong. Her hair was pale, a faint golden color and I wondered if her eyes would be fair and amber, like Hunt's, or an exotic shade I'd never seen before. Her face was delicate, heart-shaped and beautiful with full pink lips and long lashes resting on high cheekbones. She was perfect. The most beautiful female I'd ever seen. I met Hunt's pale gaze and the corner of his mouth tipped up. Was he laughing at me for checking her pulse?

Did I care?

No.

A blanket appeared over my shoulder and I unfolded it, covered her and Hunt pulled his shirt free from underneath, donned it again as I lifted her carefully into my arms, the soft material protecting her modesty and also keeping her warm.

She was soft and curvy. While I couldn't see much of her form beneath the blanket, I could feel her, the plush softness of her curves. I was eager to explore every part of her. My cock grew hard at her feminine scent.

No one would see her bare but Hunt and me. No one.

"Should we take her to the med station?" Hunt asked. "It's standard on battleships for brides to receive a medical exam upon arrival."

While I knew he was putting her wellbeing first, I found myself instantly possessive and I wanted no one, not even a doctor, to touch her. I understood the philosophy behind the exams. Most were concerned about fertility and injury during transport. The practice had become common hundreds of years ago, when transport was not so well perfected, and often, the trip through space would cause permanent damage to fragile females. But I didn't care about breeding our mate, I only cared about bedding her. Pleasing her. Easing the loneliness and pain both Hunt and I knew too well.

She was mine. Mine. No doctor would touch her. No other should see her unconscious and vulnerable. I wanted to rip the governor's eyes out for gazing upon her. I now understood what an Atlan felt like when his beast was upon him. Possessive. Protective. Unreasonable. I was being irrational, and I didn't care.

"Lady Rone was asleep after transport as well. She woke after a few minutes," Maxim told us and I relaxed a bit in relief.

"I woke in one of the exam rooms of the med floor. It was definitely an abrupt, and clinical, awakening." The lady in question had her arms crossed and a scowl on her face. "Which I doubt this young woman would care to experience."

"We thought only of your health, mate. I was there and so was Ryston," Maxim replied.

"And the doctor," Lady Rone said, countering her mate's words with a grumble. "You and Ryston were more than enough for me to handle without the doctor."

My mate was so small, so light in my arms. I stood easily. "Thank you, Lady Rone. As my mate is from Earth, I will take your advice. No doctor then. Thank you, Governor, Lady Rone, for your assistance."

The lady leaned forward, trying to peek around the blanket. "Oh, wow. She has beautiful blonde hair. And look at those cheekbones. I hate her already."

Stunned, I stared, my mind working furiously for a solution should the governor's mate decide to dislike my lady. Luckily, she grinned.

"I'm kidding, but if she's got D-cups, I'm not going to be able to be her friend."

I had no idea what D-cups were, but I would ensure my mate avoided them so she and Lady Rone became friends rather than enemies. When my mate woke, I would ask her to explain these strange threats from the governor's mate.

"While I don't doubt news of your mate's arrival will be the topic of conversation by everyone in Base 3, even the entire Colony, within the next few hours, I will let everyone know you are taking time away from your duties until tomorrow," Maxim said. *Away from your duties* was diplomatic speak for taking time to properly pleasure our mate.

Maxim slapped me on the shoulder. When I didn't move, he frowned. "Aren't you taking her to your quarters?"

I knew he spoke sense, but as I held her in my arms, the heat and scent of her filled my mind with demands, with needs I'd never felt before and had no way to combat. Hunt looked at me, a question in his eyes that I could not answer. All I knew was my cock grew hard, my thoughts hazy with lust, my feet refused to move. She was mine, and the long walk to our soldiers' quarters had never felt so far.

Her naked form haunted me and my mouth dried in anticipation of tasting her...everywhere. I glanced at Hunt, confident he would go along with the plan forming in my mind, to take her here. Now. I couldn't wait for new quarters to be assigned. I didn't want to wait and try to ease her fears with gentlemanly conversation. If she was truly mine, that wouldn't be what she needed.

Turning from Hunt, I met and held Maxim's gaze. "Thank you, Maxim. With all due respect, Governor," I turned to include Lady Rone and the two officers standing at attention near the transport controls. "All of you. Get the fuck out."

The transport controller sucked in a breath at my disrespectful language. I narrowed my eyes at him and his companion, who was grinning at me like I was the best entertainment he'd had in months. Perhaps I was. I didn't care. "Both of you. Get out. I'm claiming my mate and I'm claiming her here. Now."

Hunt, ever the diplomat, spoke up, stepping between me and Maxim, who looked at me with narrowed eyes, clearly struggling with his decision on how to handle me. But there was no handling me. Not right now. "Tyran, we can take her back to the—"

"No." I could feel the plump fullness of one breast against my palm, feel the roundness of her ass against my belly. Her scent was intoxicating, drowning me and all reason as deep instinct rose within me, and we weren't even wearing our collars. "They will leave because I am not wasting another moment to make this female ours."

Maxim laughed, took his mate's hand and ushered the controllers from their posts.

"What if a transport comes in?" one asked.

"Then the captains will be here."

The man was dedicated to his post, but in this moment, I didn't care. Transports occurred, but were few and far between. Still, I didn't want to have our mate bent over the control panel, my cock in her pussy and Hunt's in her mouth when someone arrived.

Fuck no.

"Set the transport to standby mode," I told Hunt. He looked at me with surprise before glancing at Maxim who had paused at the door when he heard me, perhaps because

I rarely gave orders—at least not since we'd been in battle. The last order I gave nearly killed us both. My battle rage had won that day, and was the reason we'd ended up in those Hive Integration caves, tortured and weak. The reason we'd ended up here.

I'd spent the last three years paying the price, doing what I was told by the governor, Hunt and the other elected commanders on the base. The deep instincts I had to command, to lead, suppressed until I was choking on them. Hunt was a good leader, deliberate, considering things from every angle and choosing the right path for the warriors here on Base 3. He was one of Maxim's most trusted advisors.

I was walking chaos. I followed orders because I chose to, not because I needed someone to tell me what to do. I followed orders of the men I respected because I didn't want the responsibility, the blood of any more warriors' deaths on my hands.

No, I didn't give orders anymore, and I saw the shock on Hunt's face—uncertain if that look was because I wanted to do this here, or because I had just barked an order at the governor of Base 3.

Maxim nodded his head in assent and left us, the door sliding closed behind the men with a nearly silent swoosh.

"She deserves a bed," Hunt grumbled, his fingers sliding over the panel. When done, he looked to our sleeping mate. "She deserves softness, Tyran. Look at her. She's so beautiful, so perfect." He looked down at his left arm, at the Hive technology that turned his arm almost completely silver, and frowned, looked at me, his gaze wandering to me. "She deserves better than us."

"She does, but she won't always get it from me. She doesn't want it," I replied.

"How the hell do you know that?"

"Because I want my collar around her neck now. I want to fuck her now. I'm not gentle, Hunt. I will demand everything from her and we will give her everything she needs. Your light and my dark."

He opened his mouth to speak, but I continued. "She's my match, Hunt. Of all the warriors on The Colony, you know me. You know the darkness I carry inside. She won't always want a bed because she's mine. She'll crave what we can give her."

He moved to stand before me, looked down at the sleeping face of the female who was now ours. "What if you're wrong?"

I narrowed my gaze. "I'm not wrong, not if she's mine."

He frowned, reached out tentatively and stroked a finger over her cheek.

She stirred then and my cock leapt to attention, her feminine scent drifting over both of us as she shifted in the blanket.

"All right, Tyran. We'll find out soon enough."

KRISTIN, *Transport Room, The Colony, Base 3*

I WAS WARM, a blanket wrapped around me the way I used to love when I was a little girl. The steady beating of a heart soothed me as I nuzzled my cheek into the hard warmth of the man holding me...

Man?

I blinked my eyes. Once, then again and my vision cleared. After that, I blinked again to make sure I wasn't hallucinating. Yes, there were two very big, very hot guys staring down at me. Warden Egara was nowhere to be seen and these men weren't human. They were beautiful, sexy, their coloring gold and brown with slightly sharper features than a human man would have. The man holding me was darker, with skin a creamy caramel, short brown hair and brown, bedroom eyes I could stare into for hours. He held me as his lighter friend touched my cheek with a gentle finger, lingering on my skin as if he was mesmerized by the sight of me.

The second had pale golden hair and amber eyes, his skin fair with just a hint of gold. His right eye held a hint of silver, and a pale silver patch of skin surrounded his eye and his right temple, the odd color disappearing beneath strands of light-colored hair.

My heart raced as I breathed in the scent of them both. Feral. Hot. So sexy my body responded as if it had just been waiting for me to pay attention, suddenly hot and aching, needy.

I tore my gaze from the men and turned my head to look around. The room was about the size of a two-car garage and utilitarian. I recognized the shiny black flooring and green grid of a transport pad from pictures I'd seen at the Interstellar Brides Processing center. A control station stood a few feet away, empty. I was alone in the room with two aliens, wearing nothing but a blanket as they stared at me like they couldn't wait to get me naked and fill me with their cocks.

And holy shit, that made me hot.

"Greetings, mate. I am Tyran." The man holding me rumbled, nuzzling the side of my head with his nose, breathing me in, his dark head a stark contrast to the pale skin of my shoulder where it peeked out from under the blanket.

Mate? Oh, wow. My entire body tensed as the reality processed. I'd known this was going to happen, but talking to the pleasant yet professional Warden Egara on Earth about taking on two dominant warriors of Prillon Prime as mates was one thing. Being here with their massive, powerful bodies towering over me?

I shivered, growing wet as they stared.

Toto, I'm not in Kansas anymore.

Hell, I'm not even on Earth anymore.

"Hello," I said, my voice a little rough. I cleared my throat and said it again.

Both of them grinned at me, but the second man answered this time, the golden one, his finger moving from my cheek to my bottom lip. "Hello, mate. I am Hunt. Your second."

The words caused the man holding me to squeeze, my two mates glancing at one another for a long moment as something passed between them I didn't understand. As if by mutual consent, they both turned and made me the center of attention once more. Tyran held me still and although I'd been in his arms for a long time, he didn't appear strained at all. That meant either I'd lost weight in transport, or he was much bigger and stronger than I first thought. I looked up at him, wiggling to get out of his arms, but he didn't set me down, shaking his head instead.

"I am Captain Tyran, mate. I am your Primary Male. Do you understand what that means?" he asked.

I thought of my conversation with Warden Egara. Oh, yes. I knew all about what this meant. He was my match, my perfect match. And Hunt was the warrior he'd chosen to help him take care of me, to have children with, to be a family. It meant two lovers making a Kristin sandwich. I shivered and licked my lips. "Yes."

He smiled then, watching my mouth as I rubbed my lips together, nerves getting the better of me. "I am yours, mate. And I admit, I am very pleased to see you." He looked at me with dark chocolate eyes, eyes I could get lost in. "Hunt is my second. He is yours as well."

Hunt smiled at me, but the look on his face was somehow softer. They were both rugged, but Hunt lacked the hard edge I sensed in Tyran, even though he had a silver eye. I wondered why Tyran was here, on The Colony. On first glance, he didn't appear to have any Inspector Gadget parts at all.

"Am I on The Colony?" I wondered. I looked around and all I could see beyond the men's large bodies was a transport room. But Tyran looked all too normal—well, normal for an alien.

"You are," Tyran answered.

The thought of what was going on under his heavy black clothing was territory a bit too dangerous for me to traverse at the moment, so I changed the subject. "God, I can't believe I just traveled to another planet. It's a little unreal."

While he didn't smile, I saw warmth in his eyes. They didn't hold mine, but roved over my face as if studying me. I didn't blame him, for I was doing the same thing to both of them, my gaze darting back and forth like a ping-pong ball, trying to come to grips with the fact that these two men were *mine*. Forever. No dating. No figuring things out. I was basically married already, and I barely knew their names.

"It was an incredibly long way and transport can be difficult if one is not prepared. Do you feel well?" Hunt asked. I could tell already he was going to be the considerate one, the one who noticed if I was hungry or cold or just needed some alone time. He made me feel safe. Cherished. Protected.

But Tyran? He looked at me like he was debating which part to bite first, and I couldn't stop the visceral reaction to his caveman attitude. His eyes were focused like lasers, dark with lust. Raw. Animal. Lust.

5

*ristin*

MY BODY CAME to life under his perusal, a wildness rising within me I didn't realize I had. The security of Hunt's presence made me worse. Somehow, I knew Hunt would stop things from going too far for me to handle, and that made me feel like being wild.

It was all insanity. I'd known them for all of three minutes, but my heart didn't care. My body didn't either. Both of them were telling my brain to shut the hell up and go with it.

I didn't feel like I'd been turned into little particles and sent through space and then reconstituted as if I were powdered milk. But I had. I should've worried about how scary the idea was, how many chances there were for mistakes. What happened if everything wasn't put back in the same place? But I didn't care, not right now. I was here, and two of the sexiest men I'd ever seen were set to devour me.

My breasts grew heavy and my nipples hardened as I imagined myself laid out between them, taking them both, four hands on my body, two mouths—one at my pussy and one suckling at my breasts—two lovers making me feel feminine, beautiful, wanted...

Okay. Really? I was a little out of control here. This needed to stop before I made a fool of myself in front of my new mates.

"Will you, um, put me down, please?" I asked Tyran, who held me so close. I needed distance if I was going to get myself back together.

I wiggled and he released my legs, but kept his other arm banded around me until I had my feet beneath me. It was then I realized I was already naked and clawed at the blanket to cover myself. We were alone in the room. While these two were my mates, I didn't know them and I wasn't quite ready to show them my body.

After tugging the blanket up to my shoulders, I spun about, faced away from them and parted the soft material enough to look down at myself.

Yes, my parts were all there. Thank God. Unfortunately, *all* of me was still there including my wide hips and overly generous curves. With this fancy transport technology, you'd think they could figure out how to do space-lipo or body sculpting. You know, just leave a few extra fat cells behind. Not like I would miss them.

What *was* missing was the landing strip I'd gotten the last time I'd been waxed. Somewhere between three, two, one and space I'd had a full Brazilian. Totally bare.

With a gasp, I lifted my hand to my head, felt the short,

soft strands of my pixie-style haircut, and sighed with relief. For a second there, I'd been afraid these weird bride protocols had taken all of it. Short and a little chubby was bad enough, but short, chubby and bald? I would have cried. Big, fat ugly-cried.

"Is everything all right?" one of the men called from behind me.

I spun back, pulled the blanket snug. Now I could see both of them clearly. They were of similar height, a similar ludicrously tall height. They had to be close to seven feet and as broad as football players. How was that physically possible? These men were from Prillon Prime. Were all males from their planet this size? If so, I looked like I'd just come from Munchkinland, not Earth.

"Do I... Do I look normal to you?" I wondered.

One frowned, the other's eyebrows went up. "Normal?" Tyran asked.

I nodded. "Yes. I'm much smaller than you guys, and we have different skin coloring and you're huge and solid muscle." All that muscle was clearly visible despite their clothing. Hunt wore what I thought might be normal clothing, pants and a tunic, not that dissimilar from things I'd seen on Earth. But Tyran was wearing some kind of body-hugging armor, a marbled black and gray that made him look intimidating as hell, like he was ready to go kill something. "You guys are huge, and strong and I'm fat and—"

"When I hear the word fat, I think of an animal that is plump for slaughter. Is this what you refer to?" Hunt tilted his head to the side, a confused look on his face.

"What?" What was he talking about? "You mean like pigs or cows?"

Tyran frowned as well, his eyes roaming over my body with an intensity that made me blush and tighten my grip on the blanket. "I was not aware there was cannibalism on Earth. Is that why you volunteered? To escape being eaten by cannibals?"

I stared at my mates with blank confusion. Were they both crazy? It seemed we were all talking in riddles. He thought we were savages on Earth? Well, perhaps we were, but we hadn't taken to eating each other. Yet. At least, not as a normal, everyday occurrence.

"No. No, I was not about to be eaten. That's not what I mean by fat." I knew my face blushed, could feel the heat rising in my cheeks that signaled a full, red-faced mortification. Two of the hottest men I'd ever seen were staring at me like I was a puzzle they couldn't solve. *No puzzle here, boys. Just feeling like a Grade-A idiot about now.*

"No one will eat you here. We are not cannibals," Hunt reassured me, his sincerity making me want to laugh. How the *hell* had we gotten into this completely insane conversation?

"Good."

Tyran took a step closer and I stood my ground. He was mine. I was going to have to work hard to remember that and not back away every time he moved in my direction. "I can't see much of you beneath the blanket. You are small, but you seem perfect to me."

"You think I'm small?" That was a new one.

They both nodded, but Hunt spoke. He seemed to be the diplomat. "You are small, but we are familiar with females from Earth, for our Queen is from your planet and so is Lady Rone, our governor's mate."

"There are other women here? On The Colony? From

Earth?" I almost dropped the blanket, so excited by the possibility of having a friend from home.

Hunt nodded. "Yes, and Lady Rone is eager to meet you."

Feeling happy, and a bit more confident, I took my time looking them over, and letting them watch me do it. "So, are all Prillon warriors this big?" I pointed at them, my bare arm coming out from the slit in the blanket.

I lifted my gaze from Tyran's thighs to where I knew his cock rested. By the thick bulge beneath his armor, he was hard for me already, and he was huge. When my attention finally returned to his face, his eyes had gone so dark they were nearly black. "Yes."

My mates were the perfect contrast standing next to one another. One light, one dark. So tall. So intense.

"We also have this." Hunt pointed to his right eye where the silver glinted at me in the harsh light of the transport room. His golden skin took on a harsher tone where the silver surrounded his eye and disappeared at the temple. I wondered how the Hive had done that to him. Wondered if it hurt.

"Does it hurt?"

He looked surprised by the question, but shook his head slowly. "No."

I looked down at the sleek floor, then held Hunt's gaze, looking into his eye. No, eyes. The silver was odd, but when I watched closely, I saw it shift and focus as he studied me. "You can see with that, can't you?"

"Very, very well. I can count the twelve freckles on your nose from here. Is that a scar on your left ear?"

I lifted my hand to my earlobe where my earring had been ripped out when I was thirteen. The skin had been split open. It had been sewn back together but there was still a faint white line.

"Wow, you're like the bionic man," I whispered.

He pointed to his right ear next. "My ear was altered as well. I can hear the blood pulsing through your body, the beat of your heart. I can count your breaths and hear the tapping of your bare foot on the floor beneath the blanket."

Whoa. I stopped tapping my bare toes on the cold, hard floor. But I couldn't stop the rest.

"Does that bother you?" he asked.

I frowned, thinking. No. It might seem strange to me for a while, but there was also something comforting in thinking Hunt would always hear me calling for him in a crowded room, or from far away. "No. Does it bother you that I'm so short? Because if it does, then we've got a problem because I stopped growing in ninth grade."

Tyran bowed, just a little, before standing again, as if offering deference to a queen. "Do not fear that I don't find you appealing. I assure you I do. Just as your desire for us grows with each passing moment. The match ensures that. The Brides Program has been used successfully for hundreds of years. You are perfect for me. The matching ensures that."

That made sense and I hadn't thought of it.

"Is it the same for you, too?" I asked Hunt.

"I am your designated second. While I am not a perfect match to you, as Tyran is, I assure you I am in complete agreement with him about his eagerness to have you here with us."

"You will not want a mate of your own?"

He stared at me for a moment as if I'd slapped him. "*You*

are my mate. Primary Male. Secondary. It changes nothing. You are mine. Do not doubt my desire for you."

I looked away, unable to hold his gaze when he was staring into my soul with those eyes. Biting my lip now, I could feel the heat spreading from my face to my neck and shoulders under their scrutiny and I shifted on my feet. "I feel strange just standing here," I admitted, feeling a little awkward and out of sorts. "Can't we go somewhere else to talk?" I tugged on the blanket, making sure it was snug around the girls. "And maybe get some clothes?" Clothes might help.

"No," Tyran said. He looked at me as if he wanted to gobble me up. "We aren't leaving here until you wear our collar and we've made you come."

I heard the word collar, but my brain short-circuited, completely focused on the word *come.*

My pussy clenched with heat and I bristled to hide my reaction. What the hell? It was like he'd just shoved a finger inside me, I was so turned on, ready to agree to almost anything. It was crazy. "Um, what? I don't think so. I didn't travel across the universe just to—" I couldn't finish the sentence. I'd be lying. I *had* come across the universe to have mind-blowing sex with my hot alien mates. And god help me, they were fucking *hot.* Panty-melting, drop-dead-gorgeous.

"Just to what?" Tyran replied. "Fuck? I didn't say anything about fucking."

"You said—"

"I want my collar around your neck. I want the taste of your pussy to coat my tongue. I want to know the sounds you make when you are lost in pleasure. I want you to know that your mates will take care of you, see to your every need."

This was a little insane. I'd been awake on a strange planet for five minutes and he wanted to get me off? Honestly, I didn't want to say no, but it just seemed *wrong* somehow. "But—"

"Drop the blanket." Tyran crossed his arms over his chest yet didn't shift his gaze from mine.

My mouth fell open at his bluntness, at the deeper timbre of his voice, but my nipples hardened and the ache grew between my legs.

"Tyran, you're being—"

Tyran cut off Hunt's words. "Our mate likes it when we take control."

"That might be true, but we should take some time, get to know each other. Give her some time, Tyran. She's not ready."

It seemed Hunt was a little more of a romantic than Tyran. Protective, too. But he was also wrong. I didn't want safe and sane right now. I felt on the edge of screaming my frustration. I needed release. I needed to be conquered, claimed by these two warriors. I needed to know they were really mine. That was the only way I was going to feel safe. Somehow, by some miracle, Tyran seemed to know that.

"I bet you're wet now, hearing your mates argue over you."

I was, but I wasn't going to admit it.

"Fuck, Tyran, I didn't know you were this..."

"What?" Tyran slowly shook his head. His tongue flicked out and slid along his full lower lip. "Dominant? Tell him, mate, tell him you want this. Tell him you need me just like this."

"How can you be so sure I do?" I asked. "I worked for the FBI. I've seen it all. I don't like women being forced. I don't like women being demeaned. I won't stand for it."

"I don't want a weak woman," Tyran replied. "We will never force you. You have a voice. You'll tell me if you don't like something." His gaze wandered over me slowly, lingering on my body like he had a direct connection to my core. "And you'll tell me when you do."

I'd never told anyone about my sexual interests. I'd known since I was younger that I was a little different than others. When my friends were playing wedding with their Barbie and Ken dolls, I was tying Barbie up. I was bending Barbie over Ken's knee for a spanking.

As I got older and learned about sex, I wanted it rough. I wanted a guy who held me down, talked dirty to me. But that didn't work so well on the old couch in my parents' basement. Steve Taylor, who'd taken my virginity, was too eager to manage anything more than breaking my hymen. He'd come in about thirty seconds. Maybe less. That was the first time he'd gotten his cock wet and he hadn't been able to hold back—even thought he'd worn a condom.

When I told my boyfriend in college I wanted him to tie me up, he'd thought I was a freak. So, yeah, he wasn't my boyfriend after that. I turned all my perverted leanings toward reading the steamier romance novels out there. Johanna Lindsay and the hero that kidnapped the virgin, keeping her prisoner on his ship. The ravaging Vikings. The commanding Doms. Those fictional heroes made me wet. They had fueled my fantasies as I used my vibrator and accepted the fact that no man would ever really be able to give me what I wanted.

I was broken. That's what I thought. Abnormal.

I couldn't tell anyone, not when I went into the FBI. Especially not after being transferred to the sex crimes division. God, if one of those guys learned I wanted to be dominated and controlled, they'd think I'd gone insane, contaminated by the sick fucks we put behind bars.

So the fantasy never became a reality and I'd never told anyone.

"How do you know what I want?" I asked.

Now he grinned, and his face transformed. God, he was so hot and that look was solely for me. Solely because of me.

"The match. We are a puzzle that has always had a missing piece. Now we've found it. Set Hunt's mind at ease."

"How?" I asked, looking to the other Prillon.

"When I commanded you to drop the blanket, did it make you hot?"

I bit my lip, stared between them.

"Never fear telling us the truth," Hunt said. "We have been outcasts for a long time. Nothing you can say will be judged here."

I took a deep breath, let it out. I'd come halfway across the universe for this. The time to be a coward was behind me. "Yes, it made me hot."

Tyran closed the distance between us, placed his big hands on my shoulders. While he was gentle, the heavy weight of them made me feel somehow settled. "Are you wet, mate? Wet and ready for my cock?"

Such gentle hands and such crude words. I shivered. "Yes."

"I'm hard. I've never been so hard. I like to dominate, be in control. Fuck hard and rough. Spank and play. I want to tie you up and make you beg, keep you exposed and open, exactly where I need you. I want to do very dirty things to you."

Oh. My. God. I was going to spontaneously combust, and he hadn't done anything but touch my shoulders. Behind him, Hunt stepped closer and I felt them surrounding me with their energy. I was completely at their mercy, and there was no one here to save me. No one who would hear me cry out. I was theirs. They owned me and there was nothing I could do about it.

The realization made my legs tremble as I fought to stay focused, not get lost in the conversation.

"What do you want, mate?"

 *ristin*

WHAT DO YOU WANT, mate?

"Everything. All of it." The words burst from me before I could stop them, my brain apparently completely disconnected from my body.

Heat flared in his eyes and the corner of his mouth tipped up.

"A perfect match."

I frowned. "The testing picked up on this...interest we share?"

"Absolutely. Will you give yourself to me, mate, to bring you pleasure you've never even imagined, in ways you've only dreamed about?"

"We don't even know her name," Hunt added. "Shouldn't we at least know that before we fuck her?"

I couldn't help but laugh then, which made Tyran's smile grow wider. It was true. I was basically giving them permission to fuck me, and I hadn't even told them my name.

Tyran stepped back so they stood side by side again. "My name is Kristin. Kristin Webster."

"Kristin, drop the blanket." Tyran's voice dropped to a deep timbre and my body responded immediately, goose bumps rising across my skin. I looked between the two, saw one who had unwavering resolve and need for me to submit. Hunt wasn't turned off, just...surprised.

These men were my mates. Two, not one, who were mine to keep. And in return, I was theirs. There was no courting, no dating. Not even a first date. This wasn't even a one-night stand. It was like finding a guy in a bar, dragging him into a bathroom, locking the door and fucking without even sharing names. But these two weren't going to leave me after we were done. They were mine. The reality of that was intoxicating. Liberating.

No, I wasn't going anywhere. Ever.

And so I did what I'd wanted to do for years and years and years. Show the real me to someone. Not just my large breasts, the heavy curves, every dimpled bit of flesh and imperfection, but also my darkest nature.

I obeyed, and dropped the blanket.

Tyran's eyes flared with dark heat and Hunt hissed out a breath.

Lifting his hand, Tyran held up three pieces of wide ribbon or...something. It wasn't metal. It wasn't plastic. It wasn't fabric. Hunt took a blue one from him, wrapped it about his neck. It had no clasps, but it somehow sealed and tightened about his neck. A collar. Tyran had mentioned it, but I'd forgotten. I watched as Tyran put a blue one about his neck as he spoke. He held one more in his hand, this one black.

"Prillon mates wear collars to show that they have been claimed and are under their warriors' protection. While we will not officially claim you until you agree and we have a mating ceremony, the collars will signify to one and all that you belong to us, just as we belong to you."

"Like a wedding ring."

"I have heard Lady Rone say something similar about your Earth custom, so yes."

"You want me to wear this?" I asked.

"You must wear it, or we cannot leave this room."

"Why?" I wondered.

It was Hunt who answered. "There are few females on the planet. You are not only beautiful, but perfect. Others will want you for their own. If you are not wearing a collar, the other warriors will assume you have rejected our claim. They will fight for your attention and the right to win you for their own."

Tyran actually growled, which made my thighs clench together. God, he was so fucking hot when he was acting like a cavemen. "That will not happen. You belong to us. No other will touch you."

"So, if I walked out of here without the collar on, it would actually start a fight?" I asked, stunned.

They both shook their heads. "No mate, your beauty could start a war," Hunt replied.

I laughed then, thinking he was exaggerating. When neither of them laughed with me, I realized they were dead serious. And they really, really thought I was beautiful.

"Is it permanent?" I wondered if, once I put it on, I'd

never be able to get the dumb thing off. I looked at the dark blue collars that now circled my mates' necks. What if this didn't work out? What if I needed to get an alien divorce—or whatever they called it out here in space?

"No. You have your thirty days to decide whether or not to accept my claim as your Primary Male. Once you choose to remain with us, we will have an official claiming ceremony. Should you decide to choose another male, the Brides Program will match you to another male for thirty days—" I couldn't miss the anger and frustration in his voice and I realized that Warden Egara had already told me all of this. I'd just forgotten. "—If that occurs, he, too, will give you a collar." Tyran blinked slowly and I felt like a bunny staring at a hungry fox. "He would be a fool not to mark you for all to see. I am not a fool."

I swallowed past the lump in my throat, both intimidated and turned on by his intensity. "What does the claiming ceremony involve?"

Tyran walked closer, bending down so his hot breath fanned my ear. "I will fuck your pussy and Hunt will fuck your ass. We will all come at the same time, all three of us, our seed deep inside you, marking you as ours."

Oh. My. God. That was hot. And really, really dirty.

Tyran lifted his hand and held a black collar out to me. He was letting me choose. He wasn't forcing me. I could say no and deep down I knew they'd be okay with that, at least until we talked it out some more.

He might be the dominant one, but I had the power. They could do nothing about me refusing the collar. They could do nothing if I refused *them*. All Tyran had said he wanted to do was give me pleasure. And I was balking?

I took the collar in my hand. It wasn't heavy, but it was cool to the touch. Lifting my hands, I put it about my neck. The ends touched at my spine and I felt them somehow join. Then the collar shrank as if it had gotten wet. It stopped once it was snugly around the base of my neck. I lifted my hand to feel the fabric, but it seemed to have meshed with my skin, the transition from flesh to ribbon nearly seamless.

A strange tingling started beneath the collar, spreading up and down my spine. A few seconds later, emotions flooded my body. Arousal. Hope. Pain. Longing. Loneliness.

Lust. Need. Desire.

My knees buckled and Hunt caught me before I crumbled to the floor.

"Oh my god!" I cried out when I *felt*. "What's going on?"

I hugged myself, all at once aroused more than I'd ever imagined. My nipples hardened, my skin became sensitive. My pussy clenched and my clit swelled. My knees almost buckled from the intensity of the feelings rushing through my body.

Hunt pulled me into his arms and I whimpered. "The collars. They create a special connection between the three of us. You are feeling what we feel."

I shuddered as the walls of my pussy clenched. Their desire. Mine. I had no idea and I no longer cared.

"I'm going to come," I replied, practically squirming in his hold. I was rubbing my legs together, trying to work my clit. My nipples pressed against the rough fabric of his shirt.

Tyran dropped to his knees before me, gripped my hip with one big hand, hooked his other behind my knee and lifted it over his shoulder. I didn't have a second to wonder what he was doing before he put his mouth on me, suckling my clit between his lips, flicking it with his tongue.

I came almost instantly, my hand tangled in and tugging at his dark hair. My head fell back against Hunt's shoulder and my eyes closed with the intensity of it. I felt it in my clit, in my empty pussy, but I also felt their desire. Tyran's ruthless need to push me. Hunt's slow burn, a desire to take his time, make me come again and again.

When I could open my eyes, I saw Hunt watching me with a mixture of desire and awe. I'd never come so quickly before in my life. And I wanted more. I was still eager, still needy. I needed to be fucked. I wasn't sure if it was my horny desperation I was feeling or theirs.

I didn't care.

"Fuck me, please." I wasn't filled with shame now. No, now I wanted to be filled with the rock-hard length of my mate's cock.

Tyran stood and I saw the glistening sign of my desire on his mouth, his chin. He licked his lips but didn't wipe the rest away.

"You aren't in charge, Kristin."

"Tyran." It was the first time I'd spoken his name, and it felt right coming from me in that breathless, imploring tone. I needed him to fuck me. I needed them to touch me. I needed more. I whimpered. Hunt's grip around my waist tightened at the sound, even as Tyran responded.

"I know. *We* know. We feel your need through the collar as well. We know exactly what you need."

"I can't fuck your pussy, mate," Hunt whispered his own dirty words in my ear as he lifted one hand to cup the full weight of my breast. "It's the Primary Mate's right to fill you with his seed, give you the first child. I will take your ass, but not today. We have to get you ready first."

"No, Hunt." Tyran's denial was confusing. Hunt must have thought so as well.

"What are you saying?" Hunt asked.

"We aren't on Prillon Prime. They've abandoned us to The Colony. We will adhere to Prillon custom and wear the collars and take a mate together, we'll both fuck her as she wants."

"But the first child is yours by right," Hunt replied.

"Any child will be ours. It matters not whose seed takes root. Does it, mate?"

I had no idea what they were talking about. But yes, I wanted kids. If they were both mine, then no, it didn't matter, did it? "No. I don't care which one of you is the biological father."

Hunt's swift intake of breath made me smile. I'd pleased him, and his happiness danced through my collar like fizzing champagne, making my head spin. I'd turned into a mind reader with the collar. No, a feelings reader.

I liked this collar. I didn't have to try to explain things to my mates. They would feel what I felt.

About a gazillion Earth divorces could probably be averted by this technology.

"You want to be fucked, mate?" Tyran asked.

I nodded my head, waited with avid and eager eyes to see his glorious body was revealed.

"Then down on your hands and knees. Show us that round ass and perfect pussy."

Hunt

I WATCHED our mate do as Tyran commanded and my cock grew harder, the pain welcome as she sank, naked, to her hands and knees. She was so small but perfect, short blonde hair caressing her jaw as her full, heavy breasts swung below her. Her ass was bare and round, the glistening lips of her wet pussy an eager sign of welcome she could not deny.

She was lustful, hot for her mates. And Tyran's orders were fuel to her sexual fire.

Tyran had always been a strong warrior, a leader in his own quiet way, but he'd been content to remain off to the side, quietly observing life upon our return from the Hive. I knew he had this in him, but he never showed it. Now? I hadn't expected his outlet, his need for control, would come through with our mate.

I shouldn't have been surprised, but I was. I *was* surprised when Kristin didn't punch him in the face at his dominance. Instead, I felt her need for it, her arousal at his commands, the peace she felt at doing his bidding. She wanted him in control. I felt the moment she relinquished her own, handed it to him like a gift. To both of us. When I watched Kristin's breathing hitch and her eyes darken with desire, I could not argue with his heavy-handed commands.

"Strip, Hunt, and lie down on your back next to her."

"What?" I tore my gaze from our mate's creamy skin to stare at Tyran. While my cock hardened at his command over our mate, having him give me orders was something new. It was unexpected and the tone of that one word question proved it.

"You heard me, second. Get on your back and free your cock. Give our eager little mate what she needs."

By the gods, that tone of voice was something new. But I couldn't deny that I wanted to do exactly what he told me. I wanted her riding me, my cock buried deep in her mouth, her ass or her pussy. I didn't care which. I wanted to taste her, as he had. The scent of her arousal was nearly driving me mad with lust. Looking at her on her hands and knees before me? I was going to come before I even got inside her.

I stripped out of my pants and tunic quickly, then took my time as I inspected our new mate. My fingers trailed along her back and shoulder, over the curve of her hip as I circled her. Her skin was so pale, such a different color than a Prillon's. Soft and warm. I didn't do as he bid, but instead remarked, "Our mate is beautiful, Tyran."

She whimpered, leaning into my touch, and I felt like a conqueror.

"On your back, Hunt. Our mate's pussy is empty."

I had no idea what Tyran had in mind, and I didn't care, content to participate as long as our mate seemed eager, and I got what I wanted. Her.

Lying on my back on the hard floor of the transport room, I didn't care that we were in a very public place with no cushion or bed beneath us. I reached over to caress one of her full breasts, the soft globe heaven in my palm. It was full and plush, heavy and the perfect handful.

"Pinch her nipple." Tyran walked around us now, his full body armor a stark contrast to our naked forms. "Pinch it hard, Hunt. Make sure she knows who she belongs to."

I hesitated until I saw Kristin's eyes heat at his words, her nipples harden into eager pebbles against my palm. I *felt* her consent, saw it when she arched her back, pressed her breast more fully into my hand. I pinched and she gasped.

"Again."

I did as commanded and Kristin moaned. Tyran leaned over, tangled his fingers in her short hair, tilting her head back and lifting her lips to his for a brutal kiss. He didn't caress her mouth with his own, he dominated, devoured her as I watched, my cock growing painful as I pinched and played with her breasts.

Tyran's lust blasted me through the collars, his need to control all consuming. Hers swirled around me next. "Now, mate, face away from Hunt and fill that wet pussy with his cock."

"You want reverse cowgirl?" she asked, looking confused.

I had no idea what she meant. Her words made no sense. What was a cowgirl?

In response, Tyran lifted her over me, easily moving her as he wished, her so small and agile. Perching her, he waited until she parted her knees and then settled her over my hips, turned so her back was to me, the perfect round spheres of her ass mine to admire as she faced away.

"Do what you're told and you'll get exactly what you want. What we know you need."

Her wet pussy rubbed the length of my cock and we both moaned, her slick essence coating me. Marking me.

"If you disobey, I'll spank you until your ass is on fire. Do you understand, mate?"

Her pussy dripped at his warning.

"Yes." The one word was nearly a whimper of need and I tried to ignore the part of my mind that was trying to figure out exactly what the fuck was happening here. I'd envisioned spreading our mate between us—on a bed—

loving her long and slow and deep, not scaring or overwhelming her with our massive frames or large cocks. But our little human didn't appear to be frightened. Not in the least. No, she was needy and desperate, her arousal and keen interest like a drug as it reached me through the collar. Addictive. She was addictive, and I hadn't even kissed her yet.

"Fuck him, mate. Take him deep."

7

*H*unt

THIS WAS INSANE. She'd arrived just a few minutes ago. We were total strangers except for the subtle familiarity from the testing and the awareness through the collars. I'd envisioned coaxing, wooing, teasing to get her into our bed. We hadn't even left the transport room and she was sliding her soaked pussy all over my cock.

Tyran paced, walking around us like a perfectionist inspecting his work. I closed my eyes when Kristin's small hand wrapped around the head of my shaft and positioned me at her hot, wet core. I gritted my teeth as she slid down my hard length, enveloping my body in her slick heat. She was so tight, a perfect fit.

I knew my pleasure must have transmitted to Tyran through the collars when he groaned and pulled the armor from his chest and shoulders, dropping it to the floor in a forgotten heap. His eyes blazed as he watched, kneeling between my legs, his gaze transfixed on the wet slide of her pussy as she lifted and sank down, my cock glistening with her juices.

"Good girl. Fuck him. Ride him. Take his seed. Make him give it to you. It's all for you."

My balls drew up, tight and heavy and ready to explode from the slick friction, the milking of her inner walls, but I held back, not ready for this to be over. Gods, I never wanted this to be over. Kristin rode me, her luscious curves a vision I could not tear my gaze from. I knew when Tyran stood and stripped the rest of his armor and boots. Knew our mate watched him, that the sight of his naked body gave her pleasure, her pussy clamping down on my cock like a fist pumping me, owning me.

Tyran stepped forward, his complete focus on our mate's face as he held his cock in front of her mouth. For a split second, I worried she'd not like the idea of sucking his cock, but I was found wrong when she opened her mouth.

"Carefully work your thumb into her ass, Hunt. Stretch her open as I fill her throat with my cock." He studied Kristin. "Do you want all your holes filled, mate?"

I blinked, shocked at his crude words, his lack of finesse in seducing our mate. But raw lust blasted me through the collar. Not his, hers. She nodded.

She wanted this. Wanted him like this. Wanted me to touch her, open her, play with her ass. Fuck her. I was to have all of her, and Tyran hadn't played with her yet, other than that one, hard kiss. He was her Primary Mate. His seed should fill her, create the first child as was Prillon custom. It was his right. It wasn't law, but the tradition went back centuries. "Tyran, you're her Primary. I don't think—"

"When we're with our mate, I'm in charge. Do it, Hunt." Tyran moved closer and our mate's mouth opened eagerly. She leaned forward and sucked him into her mouth like he was her favorite treat and she'd been starving for months. He wrapped his hands in her hair and moved, pulling back, pushing forward until I knew he was so deep down her throat she wouldn't be able to breathe.

I felt his pleasure through the collar, knew Kristin felt powerful in her ability to give that to him.

His dominance seemed to excite our mate, for she lifted her hips and slammed down on my cock, hard, opening her legs wider, taking me so deep the head of my cock bumped the hard tip of her womb with each firm stroke. The shockwave was like lightning through my body and I trembled beneath her, unable to think or deny her. This was incredible, nothing like I ever imagined.

My hands found her ass and I spread her open, gratified as she groaned, not hiding her need. I pressed into her slowly, spreading the wet heat of her arousal around my thumb until I was certain I could fill her without hurting her.

I worked my thumb carefully inside, massaging the circle of her tight muscles as she squeezed me, pussy and ass clamping down like a vise as Tyran stretched her mouth wide with his cock.

Kristin squeezed me, deep inside, using muscles only a woman can master to drive me out of my mind. I couldn't hold back, couldn't do anything but succumb. My balls drew up in a tight explosion and I came, filling her with my seed as my shout filled the small chamber.

Tyran's satisfaction was palpable, and as much as I didn't understand his need to be in command of all three of us, I had no desire to argue, not when our mate's pussy was spasming around me with her own release. I felt her come around my thumb as her entire body pulsed and exploded. Her scream was muffled by Tyran's cock and he groaned.

Pulling free of her mouth, Tyran didn't even let her catch her breath. He lifted her off me and I let her go, curious where his wild claiming would go next.

"Sit up, Hunt."

I was done arguing, or trying to figure him out. I sat, and Tyran turned Kristin about to face me, then lowered her to her knees in front of me. Her eyes were glazed with pleasure, her pink lips swollen and plump from the pressure of being wrapped around his cock.

He fell to his knees behind her and with a quick shift of his hips, thrust his cock up into her pussy. She gasped, her head thrown back to rest on his chest even as her arms reached for me to steady her.

"Yes. God. Do it. Fuck me." Her demand was silky and hoarse, her skin flushed a dark rose as he filled her, thrusting over and over hard enough to make her breasts bounce and her breath catch in her throat. She looked at me, her pale eyes blurry, yet intense. She *saw* me, *felt* me. Felt both of us.

"Suck her tits. Play with her clit. But if she talks again, makes any demands, stop."

My lips were around nipple, sucking her deep, before he'd finished talking. I felt the little bud harden on my tongue. And gods, she tasted even better than I'd hoped, all soft and feminine and mine.

I couldn't stop the growl that came from my throat as I thought the word. She might be matched to Tyran, but she was still mine. My seed coated her pussy, easing his way. My hands were on her body. She was trapped between me and Tryan, and I realized it didn't matter who was first and who was second. She was ours.

Dropping one hand to her wet folds, I found the sensitive nub and stroked her, pinched and plucked, careful to pull back, to stop before she could find release until she bucked against Tryan's arm around her waist, desperate for something Tyran had not decided to give her yet. Yes, I saw what Tyran was doing, pushing her to the brink of pleasure, making it stronger, more intense, *amazing.*

She whimpered, her hands clawing at my chest, leaving marks I would wear like badges of honor. No ReGen wand would be allowed to heal them. Should the doctor try, he'd receive a fist to his face. They were mine, as she was.

"Do you want to come, mate?"

"Yes. Please!" She tried to use her legs to gain leverage, but Tyran was too strong, his arm banding about her waist, holding her to him, holding her up. Holding her exactly where he wanted her. An Atlan beast couldn't defeat him in raw strength. Our small, fragile female had no hope of breaking his hold, or his will.

He leaned forward as I played with her clit, rolling it slowly between two fingers as his lips traced the curve of her ear. "Do you want me to fill you up? Fuck you? Let Hunt rub your sensitive little clit until you come all over my hard cock?"

She shuddered, her eyes drifting closed. I didn't like that. I wanted to watch her come apart, as Tyran had moments ago. I wanted to see the fire in her eyes.

"Open your eyes, mate." My voice was deep like Tyran's and had the sharp bite of command.

Her eyelids lifted and I held her gaze as Tyran shifted

under her, lifting her up with the slow, hard glide of his cock filling her from behind again and again. "Watch him, mate. Don't try to hide from us. We know everything. We feel everything you feel. We know what you need and we'll give it to you. We'll give you everything."

"Yes." She licked her lips and my cock swelled in response. Already, I wanted her again.

"Then come, mate. Come for us." Tyran stopped holding back, pumping into her like an untamed beast as I worked her clit. She shattered in seconds, screaming her release, but that wasn't enough for Tyran, his barked command that she come again all the more shocking when she did. I felt it rolling through her, unstopping.

Tyran gave in at last, his release hitting me through the collar like an ion blast as he filled our mate's pussy with his seed. She had taken both of us, any child we created would truly be ours now as we would have no way of knowing who had sired it. But that was fine with me. I didn't care. Kristin was ours. She was beautiful. Sensual. Like wildfire in our arms.

Tyran pulled his cock free and she slumped forward, into my embrace. I caught her and cradled her to me as Tyran brought over the long-forgotten blanket. We wrapped her up and once he was sure she was settled, protected and sheltered in my arms, he turned away without a word to don his armor.

Kristin was ours, but I worried as I never had before that Tyran might never truly be hers, that he might be too broken, too dark for even her softness and light to reach.

ristin

I GASPED and sat straight up. The room was dark and I had no idea where I was. A dream lingered, but it was forgotten, becoming blurry and slipping away even as I tried to remember. My bedroom had a window to the right of my bed. I rolled over, looking for the shine of the neighbor's porch light surrounded by a dark silhouette, but the window wasn't there. The bedding felt different, too. Softer. And the floral scent of my fabric softener was noticeably absent. Instead I smelled musk, and man and sex.

While I wasn't exactly afraid of the dark, I kept a nightlight on in the bathroom. I'd stubbed my toe one time in the middle of the night stumbling to pee and I'd never wanted to do that again. But no light filled the space. I could feel the walls of the room, the ceiling pressing down on me, but I couldn't see them. I couldn't see anything. Not one piece of furniture. No door. And, I was naked, my bare breasts and shoulders slightly chilled because the sheet lay draped over my waist. I usually slept in a t-shirt and panties. But nothing about this was *usual.*

Shifting my legs, a twinge of soreness pinged my system from my core. I was sore. The pain flooded me with memories and everything came back to me in a rush, as if my brain had just needed a few extra seconds to wake up. Why hadn't I felt the soreness in my body first? My muscles were tight and achy and my pussy was tender. So was my ass. When I moved, my thighs rubbed and the lingering stickiness added friction to the normally smooth glide of skin on skin. My nipples hardened with an unfamiliar ache at the rough sexual play I suddenly couldn't get out of my mind. I felt well used. Needed. Owned.

My mates had left no doubt about how much they wanted me and I'd never felt so appreciated, nor desired in my entire life. The feeling was heady and I had to work to hold in a giggle at the complete insanity of my new life.

I was on another planet, with not one mate, but *two.* And I'd let them do whatever they wanted to do to me. Hell, I wanted more now.

Lifting my hand to my collar, I breathed a sigh of relief when I felt the smooth material under my fingertips, the mark of Prillon mates yet another reminder of where I was. I closed my eyes, suddenly feeling bereft. I couldn't feel Tyran anymore. His intensity earlier had been like a slow-burning lava moving through my system. And my second, Hunt. He was calm, the balm to cool Tyran's fire. Without him, I wasn't sure I could deal with his dominant nature, his complete need for control. Logically, I realized he needed my trust, needed me to submit to him. But if I was perfectly honest with myself, I wasn't sure I could do it without the assurance of Hunt's calm control. Tyran had made me feel like a wicked, wild, reckless, crazy lover. I'd never been so turned on in my entire life. But I'd been scared, too. Afraid of him. Even more afraid of myself.

Hunt's cool reserve had been my anchor, and I pondered the wisdom of an alien computer system. Somehow, the Interstellar Brides processing protocols had mated me with two warriors that balanced one another perfectly. Light and dark. Fire and ice. Reckless and reserved. By some miracle, a computer had known I would need them both.

Speaking of mates, where were mine? I had no idea what time it was. Whether it was night or day. All I knew was I was wide awake and starving.

Pulling the sheet up to my chest, I sat up and scooted toward what I thought was the edge of the gigantic bed. I realized it was the biggest I'd ever seen, more than large enough to hold one human woman and two seven-foot Prillon warriors. I found the edge and swung my feet over the side and my toes didn't reach the floor. Nope. I wasn't in my bedroom. Hell, I wasn't even on Earth.

I was about to jump down and take my chances when part of the wall slid silently open, like on Star Trek. There was no *door*, no doorknob or creaky hinges. A section of the wall slid sideways and disappeared. And there, with light shining behind him like he was some kind of god, was the silhouette of one very big, very broad Prillon warrior. His emotions hit me immediately. Contentment. Curiosity. Concern.

"Hunt."

He heard his name and his emotions spiked to

possessive. Protective. Primal. Maybe he wasn't so cool and in control after all.

"I felt you wake, Kristin. I feel your hunger."

Maybe I should have been freaked out by that statement, but the wild bout of fucking had gotten rid of most of my insecurities. The collar made the three of us extremely sensitive to each other. It definitely ratcheted up the pleasure factor. When I was with a new guy, I often couldn't get out of my head, worried he'd think me a perv or a slut for liking sex a little too much. I got off on a guy taking control. Off spankings. Off toys. Off a little back door action. I liked it rough. I'd discovered that while a lot of guys might like to fantasize about a woman like me, once we were naked together, when the shit got real, I was often too much for them to handle.

But I wasn't too much for Hunt and Tyran. No way. Tyran pushed me to my limits, limits I hadn't even known I had. Hunt had been a little stunned, I'd felt it, when Tyran pushed me. It seemed he hadn't known his own friend's personal brand of kink. But Hunt had joined in happily enough and I knew they both got off on it. On all of us doing all that wild stuff.

A rumble escaped Hunt's chest as I became aroused again, just by thinking about riding his cock. Of Tyran giving us both orders, pulling my hair. Hunt stepped into the room as I shivered. "Lights, ten percent."

The room brightened just enough for me to see him, to notice he wore dark clothing and that his gaze was roving over every inch of me, but not much more.

"Do you know how beautiful you are?" he asked, a burst of need flaring in my collar to accompany his words.

I shouldn't have been embarrassed by the question,

especially since I *felt* the truth behind it, but I was, and I tugged the sheet up to my neck.

"Don't," he said, coming over to sit on the side of the bed, the mattress dipping from his weight. "I know I'm not commanding like Tyran and I never will be, but I hope you will come to care for me as well."

For such a formidable figure, I heard the uncertainty in his voice.

"I already do." I leaned over and rested my head on his shoulder. I knew he would hear the truth in my words as I'd felt the truth in his. "I need you, too, Hunt."

He turned his head to look down on me and I gathered my courage, lifting my lips to offer a slow, gentle kiss. I let the sheet slip, let it fall back to my waist. He kissed me slowly, tenderness and affection in the touch. When he pulled back, he stared at my breasts, then offered me a smile. "You can't blame a warrior for looking. You truly are lovely and I am still amazed you are mine."

"And you are mine." I had to say it out loud. This whole thing still felt like a dream. I was half afraid I was going to wake up in the stupid chair on Earth with Warden Egara blinking down at me like a wise little owl, ready to scold me for fighting – for not wanting to go back.

"I felt your upset, mate." Hunt lifted his hand and stroked my cheek. "Tell me what bothers you."

"I woke up in the dark and had no idea where I was. I was confused, but seeing you, it settles me. I feel... safe," I admitted to him.

"No harm will ever come to you, Kristin of Earth. We will protect you with our lives."

I knew that. I didn't have to hear the words or feel the full impact of it through the collar.

He lifted the hand farthest from me and had a strange looking wand in his grip, the tip a strange blue coil that glowed in the dark room. "This is a ReGen wand. It will heal you."

A strange, very faint buzz seemed to come from the thing and I leaned back, trying to get away from it. "I'm fine."

"No. We were rough with you." He frowned at that statement and I felt doubt cloud his mind. Worry. About what, I wasn't sure, but I wanted to ease him. I nodded and he moved the wand closer to me, holding it just a few inches from my skin as he started at my head and worked his way down my entire body. My chafed nipples stopped burning and the soreness between my legs faded to nothing as it passed.

"Wow." I would have loved to have one of those back on Earth a time or two. Like when I fell out of the swing and broke my arm in third grade. Or the first time I'd been cold cocked during hand-to-hand training at Quantico. "Thank you."

"Anything, mate. Anything you need, you have only to ask."

"I need a shower. And food. In that order." The ache was gone, but the scent of sex and sin clung to my skin like hell's own perfume. "And why can't I feel Tyran anymore?"

Hunt swallowed. Hard. "He's too far from us at the moment. He's out checking on our new warriors."

"Oh." I was bummed. I missed him, but I wasn't going to say it. Apparently, Hunt *felt* it. Pain and disappointment flooded my collar.

"I will take you to him." He stood, not looking at me and I couldn't let him walk away. Not feeling like that. Reaching forward in a rush, I grabbed his huge hand and pulled back, stopping him.

"Hunt, the testing matched me to Tyran, but there's a reason Tyran chose you to be my second. I need you, too."

His gaze met mine. The color was striking. I'd never seen caramel eyes before, but I was mesmerized. By him.

He shook his head. "No, mate. Tyran could have chosen from dozens of others. Any of them would have been honored to care for you, to cherish you."

I squeezed his hand. It was so big, proof that we were so very different.

"No. After what we did last night, what Tyran just... knew about me, about what I wanted—no, what I *needed*— it's obvious the processing protocols work. He knew things about me that others have never understood. He knows, and he needs me, too. He needs me to be what I am. I don't have to hide. I don't want to hide. The testing really makes the whole getting-to-know-each-other phase much easier."

He frowned, but he was listening so I continued.

"Tyran made you his second because of who you are. He needs you. You two balance each other out and that means that I need those same traits. I don't want two mates who are bossy as fuck, who ride the razor's edge all the time. I like to be dominated in the bedroom, yes, but I also like this. You. Me. I like to feel safe. I need stability just as much as I need Tyran's passion. I need you making me feel like this. Cherished and protected." My smile was shy and I batted my eyes at him. I'd never, ever had this kind of conversation with a man before. But he wasn't a man. He was an alien, and my mate. He was mine. "You're kinda sweet, Hunt, and I'm not giving you up. If Tryan's going to break me, I need you here to put me back together."

He smiled then. "Always, mate." He lowered his hand to my neck and pulled me to him for a slow-burn kiss before releasing me. I swayed on my feet and he laughed, grabbing my hand again with an easy familiarity that would have taken months, if not years, of dating on Earth. I knew my arousal, my complete surrender, was his to claim if he wanted it. And I knew he could feel my desire for him through the collars. "If you tell anyone I'm sweet, I'll spank your ass and I won't need Tyran to tell me to do so."

I blushed at the thought of my gentle giant making my flesh burn. "I'll keep it a secret." I was quiet for a moment, just staring at our joined hands, but one image circled in my mind, haunting me. Tyran. Silent Tyran. His heart heavy with a darkness I didn't understand. Leaving me. Leaving us. "Tyran...," I began.

Hunt sighed. "Tyran, like me, fought for the Coalition and was captured by the Hive. Each and every warrior on The Colony was a prisoner at one point. We all escaped, but we endured our own horrors. The torture each of us suffered was different."

I reached up with my free hand and caressed the silver skin at Hunt's temple, stared into Hunt's silver eye. He shuddered and closed his eyes, leaning into my touch as if I'd offered ambrosia straight from the gods. I stroked the flesh with my thumb, finding it to be slightly cool to the touch, but the change in temperature was hardly noticeable. I soothed my mate and realized I had absolutely no idea what the Hive had done to Tyran. "What did they do to him?"

His eyes opened slowly, as if reluctant to face such a morbid question. "Tyran is unlike any other warrior I know. They didn't mark him on the outside. I think they wanted to send him back to us, to fool our commanders into thinking he was untouched."

"But he's not?"

"No." Hunt turned his head and placed a kiss in the center of my palm. "Tyran's muscles and bones have been infiltrated."

I tried to imagine what that meant and couldn't. "So? What does that mean?"

Hunt sighed and pulled away and I felt guilt running through him like a river. Guilt that he was here, with me, receiving pleasure while Tyran suffered. It was my stubborn mate's own damn fault. If Tyran hadn't walked away, I'd be petting him right now, too. But he hadn't let me.

"His body is strong, abnormally strong and fast. He's stronger than an Atlan in beast mode. I saw him pull apart the hull of a fighter with his bare hands, shredded the metal like it was paper." Hunt paused to let me process, but not long enough. "Most of us have one or two places on our bodies scarred by the Hive, like me with my eye and my arm. We have small scars. But Tyran's entire body is Hive. He has microscopic implants in every muscle and every bone. He has to be careful every moment of every day. And he has to be very careful of you."

"Why me?"

Hunt laughed then, his amusement genuine. "Because you, mate, are small and fragile and perfect. You're a flower petal under our boots and as badly as we long to touch you, we are always aware of how easily you might be broken."

So, I'd been having sex with some kind of Superman who could rip through sheets of metal with his bare hands?

My stomach growled a reminder that I hadn't eaten in over a day and I shook my head. Whatever. I wanted him. I needed him. I was hungry and mad and I didn't care what kind of fucked up mental games these warriors were playing with themselves on this planet. He was mine, microscopic parts or not.

"He's mine. I don't care what he is. I was matched to the way his is *now*. You're both mine, and I'm not giving either of you up."

"While I remember what happened to me, I don't let it rule me. I have accepted the change. Some cannot and they kill themselves. Some become aggressive. Others acclimate over time, their anger diminishing as the months pass. Tyran, well, his failure haunts him more than most."

"Why?" Was that the only word I could speak today?

"He's a Zakar."

I opened my mouth to give him the two-year-old's favorite question one more time, but he cut me off.

"The Zakar family is a very important family on Prillon Prime. They have commanded the Fleet in Sector 17 for more than six hundred years. His cousin, Grigg, was made commander of the battlegroup a few years ago, the youngest commander in over a century."

The lights were coming on in my mind, slowly. "What does that have to do with Tyran?"

Hunt sighed. "My family is not of the elite class, so I don't feel the pressure Tyran does. His family is—difficult. Full of warriors who served, who fought for many, many years. Even their women are ruthless and cold. His family cut off all contact when he was taken by the Hive. His lands and wealth were given to his sister. He is dead to them."

Dead to them? My whole body clenched with pain. "What assholes."

Hunt held my gaze. "Now you begin to understand.

Coalition fighters are captured and contaminated. Should we survive Hive torture, we are sent here to live out our lives. We were denied mates, denied family, our wealth gone. Our homes, gone."

"But I'm here."

He stroked my cheek. "Yes. Thank the gods, our new Prime is one of us. He understands and is trying to help. But hope is fragile, Kristin. You are only the second mate to arrive to The Colony even though our warriors began testing nearly six months ago. Your arrival is a miracle. And the fact that you will be a bride of Zakar—here—" He cut himself off as if he didn't know how to finish that sentence.

"So, Tyran doesn't want a mate?"

"He wants you so badly it is destroying him. When he is in pain, he just gets... quiet."

Quiet? Was that what they were calling it these days?

"Don't you mean highly sexual and extremely dominant?"

Hunt shrugged. "It is one way he copes. He lost control when he was at the mercy of the Hive, so it's understandable that someone like him would become even more tempered. He preferred to be in control before he was captured, but he needs it even more now. You help with that, giving him an environment where he can wield power."

"Sex, you mean."

"Exactly. By submitting, you give back his strength. It's beautiful to watch."

"If it's so beautiful and helpful, why is he not here? Why can't I feel him? Why did he walk away?" I raised my free hand and touched the collar. "I don't care about his family. Like I said, they sound like assholes."

"When he's working through something in his mind, he

works. He hasn't come back to our quarters. Maybe he regrets what he did with you, how he acted. Maybe he's just taking time to think. It doesn't matter, Kristin. He'll figure things out. I know you're good for him. For us."

I wrapped my arms around him and melted into his embrace, the sheet completely forgotten. I looked up at him, my chin resting on his chest. "I'm glad I'm here."

He kissed me then, slow and sweet. When he pulled back, I grinned. I felt our shared amusement through the collar. "I'm not sweet, mate. Do not forget this very important fact."

I grinned. "Our little secret."

"I want you," he admitted, his hands running slow, seductive strokes up and down my bare back. "There are no rules against a second taking his mate and giving her pleasure, but you need to bathe and eat. And I want Tyran here with us when I take you again."

I understood. We were still too new, too raw. We needed to be three together. "Yes. Should we go find him?"

"Let's get you some clothes from the S-Gen and I will take you on a tour. I have no doubt word will get back to Tyran about *where* you are." He looked me over, his eyes lingering in places that made me tingle. "You go take a shower and then we'll go meet the others."

"The others?"

He leaned forward until our foreheads met. "Yes. Remember I said you are only the second bride to arrive on The Colony? Meeting you will give many of the other warriors hope. They will see you glowing with happiness, because of our mad fucking abilities."

I rolled my eyes, playfully punched him in the chest, but it was as hard as the wall behind us. I opened my mouth to debate his point, but found I could not. Yes. I was happy, and it had been because of them. For the first time in a long, long while, I was happy, without a care in the world. I wasn't worried about some thirteen-year-old girl who'd gone missing, dealing with scared parents, the good-old-boys club or evil criminals. It was just me and my mates. And I knew Tyran was mine. Hunt was mine. They weren't going anywhere and neither was I. We'd figure it out. "Yes. I am happy."

He pulled back and looked me over once more, the grin on his face full of mischief. "I guess we'd better make sure you're wearing blue."

I blinked slowly, trying to connect the dots. "Why?"

Hunt pulled me along and I followed as he led me to the bathing room. "Because blue is Tyran's family color. He'd lose his mind if he saw you wearing something else in a room full of unmated warriors."

ristin

"SOMETHING ELSE? LIKE WHAT?"

Hunt chuckled. "Like Governor Rone's copper. Or Prime Nial's dark red."

I smiled back. "Maybe we should shake up his world a little bit." I was mad, mad at Tyran for taking me so thoroughly and then walking away. Angry that he'd left me without explanation or a kiss good-bye. I wanted to push his buttons. He needed someone to push him and I was more than happy to do the job. I'd never backed down from a challenge before. I wasn't about to start now. "I've always looked spectacular in red."

My second swatted my naked bottom as I hurried to the shower. "The only thing red on you is going to be the color of your ass when we're both done with you."

Heat flared in my body of them taking control again, which made Hunt growl.

"Not today, mate. No pushing Tyran . He'd have my head. Once your collar is blue, you can have all the fun you desire tormenting your poor, helpless mate." His gaze darkened as the water turned on, hot and steamy and smelling like heaven with a mix of cleansing agents they'd told me the water contained. "But you'd better be prepared to face the consequences." He gave me another playful swat.

I stepped under the water with a grin on my lips. Consequences? Like a sound spanking? Or a bossy alpha male bending me over and filling me up? Or shoving me against the wall, ripping my clothes off and fucking me until I begged for release? Or perhaps ordering my second to hold me captive in his arms while Tyran filled me from behind? Oh, yes. I could live with *consequences* like that.

I bathed and dressed quickly, standing on the odd S-Gen pad, a smooth black structure in the corner of the living quarters. A bright green light scanned my body and I stepped down when Hunt told me to. To my delight and fascination, I watched as a matching set of pants, tunic and soft soled boots appeared on in the middle of the pad, as if they'd been transported from a store. They fit perfectly, the fabric clinging without being too tight, as if it had been made for me. The tunic had sleeves that fell to just above my elbows, the neckline was cut to highlight and draw attention to my collar, dipping and swirling just below the black ribbon, and the tunic fell to mid-thigh, covering my ass so I didn't feel like all the junk in my trunk was going to be on display.

The clothes were, as Hunt insisted, the same dark midnight blue of his and Tyran's collars, but I really didn't mind. I liked knowing they wanted to shout to the world that I was theirs.

I was just pulling on the second boot when some kind of speaker next to the door exploded with sound.

"Captain Hunt! We need you now! There's been an attack!"

I slammed my foot in the boot and stood as someone pounded on the door. Hunt waved his hand over the control panel and the door slid away to reveal four armed warriors in full armor, like Tyran had worn the day before. "Captain, the governor commands you and Lady Zakar to meet him in command. Now."

"Is Lady Rone there?" I blurted, before Hunt could stop me. I assumed that I was Lady Zakar. Another change I'd have to get used to.

The warrior looked at me, his eyes drinking me in now that he had permission. He was staring, but not in a creepy way. More like fascination, or awe. Like I was a ghost or an angel about to disappear. "Yes, my lady."

Hunt turned to me and I could see the order forming on his face. He was turning from gentle mate to hardened leader before my eyes. I shook my head, knowing what he was thinking. "Nope. No way, Hunt. I'm going. I was in law enforcement on Earth. I'm going, and I want one of those guns." I motioned to the four guards, each of whom carried a full sized rifle of some sort. The warriors were all like my mates, Prillon, their skin ranging from dark gold to a dark brown, nearly the color of black coffee. They were huge and intimidating as hell. I really, really wanted that gun.

Holding out his hand to me, he relented. "I don't have time to argue and the governor wants you there. Stay close." He frowned. "But *no gun*."

Satisfied, for the moment, I took his hand. But I eyed the thigh holsters on two of the warriors as we walked behind them down the hall. There were smaller, silver space guns of some kind strapped to their legs. They couldn't be *that* much different than my standard issue Beretta. Before the day was over, one of them was going to be mine.

Tyran, Base 3, Command Room

SEEING my mate so happy meeting Lady Rone was the only thing keeping me from ripping the heads off of every male in the room as if I were an Atlan beast. I felt Kristin's relief at meeting someone else from Earth, at not being the only female. I would remember this moment when we were too much for her. Two Prillon warrior mates would be a difficult transition even for a Prillon female. But one from Earth, where I knew the men were much smaller? I'd fought beside human warriors. They were brave and fierce, and at least a head shorter than either Hunt or myself.

Hunt and I had to be much more than Kristin probably expected.

But she'd done well with us, between us, taking our cocks and staking a claim of her own. Thank the gods for the collars. They'd allowed us all to push through questions that, because of the strip about our necks, need not be answered. I didn't have to wonder if I was making my mate happy at any given moment. What others would be forced to guess, were, for us, givens. Add to that the testing match and I felt confident where Kristin was concerned. I watched her every move, the smallest change in her body or her expression. My obsession combined with the knowledge I gained about her emotions and needs through the collars fed my confidence in her, in our match.

What I was not so calm about was me.

I was a threat to anyone who stepped near her. I would rather kill myself than hurt my mate, and I'd used every ounce of my control to keep my strength at bay when we were together. I'd been rough and commanding, but I had been gentle. I'd come back from my time with the Hive as less Prillon and perhaps more beast. I didn't know my own strength and I had a hair trigger control. I'd been deliberate in guarding my emotions, always remaining on the periphery, watching, following Hunt's lead these last three years.

Hunt led. I kept myself in check. It was a system that had been working perfectly.

Until now. Now, I was hanging on by the thinnest of threads, one leer or pleasant smile by one of the warriors and I was going to turn into a berserker. She looked so beautiful in my colors. I was proud to see her in the dark blue, even if my family, those who the color honored, did not care about me any longer. Hunt, Kristin and I would make our own family, just as soon as her collar matched ours.

Kristin Webster of Earth brought out the best in me. And the worst. She was light, even her hair and skin were like the suns in the sky. She wore her hair shorter than Rachel, but I found I preferred it and the unobstructed access to the delicate skin of her neck. Even now, I could not stop staring at the long line of her throat, the soft curve of her jaw. I wanted to kiss her there, over and over, for hours.

Her smile alone made my heart clench. Knowing what was beneath the tunic? Well, that was what kept me hard and made me a jealous, possessive lunatic. Which didn't bode well for the lifespans of the others in the room should they hurt her.

Which they wouldn't. It didn't mean I had to like the men ogling her, wanting her.

She was mine.

As if she sensed my internal chaos—she probably did— she glanced my way, held my gaze and smiled with a feminine curve of her lips that spoke of a shared secrets. Desire. Promises made. Yes, she was mine.

And so I clenched my hands into fists and leaned against the wall, listening. I needed to keep several yards away from her, from the others. If I was going to murder some warriors, I didn't want to do it with the governor and his mate in the room.

But if Hunt's second-in-command didn't stop eyeing Kristin—

"How many have gone missing?" Maxim asked.

That distracted me from the other warriors' annoying fascination with my mate.

"One more today. That makes five in two months."

"So, it's only my men? All new warriors to The Colony?" Hunt asked. He was in his element. This was where he was in control, in command. While Maxim was the governor of Base 3, Hunt was in charge of all the new arrivals. He cared for their transition, for their futures. With some just disappearing as if they'd been transported away, this was his problem. His men.

He might be my second in the bedroom when we took Kristin, he was the primary here. When he gave commands, even I followed them. And so I listened to the latest updates on the odd happenings, and kept an eye on Kristin. Even with the governor's personal guards about, she was still mine to protect.

"Yes, and we don't know why or what's happening to them," the governor's second, Ryston, answered.

"That can't be a coincidence," Hunt said, crossing his arms over his chest. While we were in the command room, no one sat. Everyone was too tense after discovering a now-obvious pattern. Something was fucking wrong here on The Colony and we had to start putting the puzzle pieces together. "Lieutenant Perro is new here, and I assigned him to Section 9."

Lady Rone remained quiet, listening until now. "Find Krael and you'll find your missing men."

The governor looked at his mate. "We don't know that yet."

"I do," she muttered, and I felt a flair of humor from Kristin. She found Lady Rone's comments amusing for some reason. I had no idea why that would be the case.

"Perro was assigned to Section 9 with the other new arrivals. We've had three disappearances from that section in as many weeks." Hunt seemed unaffected, as always, but I knew the truth now that we were linked to each other and our mate through the collars. He was just as edgy as I, his mind clouded with lust. I had no idea how he continued to form coherent sentences, but he did. "We should start the search there."

"I want to go with you," Kristin said. Her voice held none of the wariness of being a new arrival on the planet. She was in command of herself and I felt her confidence as well through the collar.

"No," Hunt and I said at the same time, but while his voice was level and controlled, mine was like a barked command. Several heads turned my way. It was the first thing I'd said since I entered the room.

"I was an FBI investigator on Earth. I worked in human trafficking." She turned to argue her point to the governor, but her efforts were wasted. I was not going to let her go out chasing Hive, and neither was Hunt. "I searched for people who were kidnapped and sold into slavery. While I doubt that is what happened to your warriors, I do know how to search for them."

Hunt shook his head where he stood beside her, his arms crossed over his chest. "Absolutely not. You don't know the planet or the way these warriors think. Nor are you familiar with our enemy. If there are traitors working for the Hive on this planet, they'll be extremely dangerous. And they won't think or act like those from Earth."

"You were in the FBI?" Lady Rone asked Kristin.

Our mate nodded. "I trained at Quantico, but I worked all over, wherever a case took me. I dealt with Columbian drug dealers, bankers from Hong Kong, Mexican cartel leaders, even the Russian Mafia. I find people. People who are in trouble, taken against their will. It's what I do. I can be helpful here."

Lady Rone offered her a smile, then looked to Hunt. "I can vouch for her experience on Earth. You may not appreciate the depth of her skills, but I can. She saved innocents from the dregs of society. She can do it here, too."

Maxim put a hand on his mate's shoulder. She looked up at him. "She can help," she said to him.

"It is not my decision, Rachel. She is not my mate." He looked to Hunt. "You will take four guards and go to Section

9. Work your way around the entire outer perimeter. Report back every hour."

Hunt nodded, pointed to four of his warriors. They preceded him out of the room and Kristin stopped Hunt with a hand on his arm. "I can help. Truly."

"The answer is no, mate." He stroked her cheek, then looked to me. "Tyran."

He leaned down, kissed Kristin on the top of the head, then left the room, the door sliding shut behind his group.

I felt Kristin's anger pulsing at me. She was furious at being disregarded, but neither of us could allow her into danger. We'd just found her. She had no idea how truly rare and precious she was.

She stomped over to one of the other guards, held out her palm. "Give me your gun."

Her eyes lowered to the thigh holster and the ion pistol secured there.

The Atlan looked down at her with wide eyes. He was even bigger than me and I approached, ready to protect my mate from the beast within him.

"Do you know how to use one?" he asked, a small smile playing at his lips.

"Don't patronize me. I might be small, but I know how to shoot. I know how to kill."

Kristin had killed before. I felt it, felt the cold chill of that truth and her strength made my cock harden. All that fire, that power, and she surrendered it to me.

"You will not take the Atlan's weapon," I told her, approaching. I placed a possessive hand on her shoulder. If the Atlan had any doubt she was mine, if the collar and the blue tunic were not enough, this would help. I only hoped that she still had our scent on her skin. Had she washed away our seed? I hoped not. I wanted the beast to scent our possession of her, know the truth.

She was ours.

"Lady Zakar, I do not wish to offend. As the governor said, if your mate wishes you to have a weapon, then it is his decision, not mine." He bowed and stepped back. Thank fuck I didn't have to challenge him.

Kristin turned her narrowed gaze on me. "*Your decision? You're going to deny me the ability to help? What am I supposed to do, sit around all the time barefoot and pregnant and cook your dinner and rub your back after a long day at work?*" She pouted like a little girl, pursing her lips out at me. I might have fallen for the ruse if I hadn't felt her fury blasting me through the collar. "So, what is my job going to be here? Is my only job to fuck you and Hunt? Because you can use a blow up doll for that."

I heard the warriors murmuring around us, but I didn't turn my gaze from her. I wasn't trying to make her angry, I just couldn't give her what she wanted. I couldn't allow her to risk her life, not for this.

"You are new here, Kristin. While we are well and truly matched, there is still much to learn. I had no idea about your function on Earth until now. I am impressed with your efforts, but it is my job—and Hunt's—to keep you from harm. We are all here on The Colony because of the Hive, what they did to us. I will not let that happen to you. I cannot hand you a weapon and encourage you to walk into danger, to risk your life."

"There's danger everywhere. Hell, this ceiling could fall in and hurt me. I'm a grown woman, you can't protect me from everything."

"It is my greatest honor and privilege to try."

She didn't understand the depth of a Prillon's possession. She saw it as oppression instead of devotion. But I would convince her. I would make her understand.

Pursing her lips, she narrowed her eyes. She was fast. I had to give her that. She had my weapon from my holster and her fingers wrapped around it before I could blink. Turning, she headed toward the door. It opened for her, but she didn't make it a foot outside before I scooped her up in my arms, tossed her over my shoulder.

10

"TYRAN!" she cried, hitting my back with her fists. I felt the hard metal of the ion pistol. I just had to pray she didn't shoot someone accidentally before she learned how to use it.

"Governor," I said, looking over my shoulder. Thankfully, he knew what I wanted and closed the distance.

"Lady Zakar, if I may." His words matched his actions. While I couldn't see what he was doing, I knew he was taking the weapon from her hands. I would allow only Maxim or Ryston to touch my mate, for they had one of their own and I knew the union to be strong. I had no reason to be jealous of the governor. The other warriors...

"Put me down! You're behaving like a stupid caveman."

I had no idea what she was talking about, but I was behaving a touch irrationally. Hunt had to do his job, so it was mine to protect her while he was gone. Her feistiness, her eagerness to charge into the fight, to help find the lost members of our community was heartening. She wanted to help.

But not at the expense of her safety. The fact that she would face down an Atlan warrior, and then have the fucking balls to take my own weapon out of its holster and point it at me should have made me angry. Instead, it made me hard. So fucking hard there was only one thing to do.

I walked down the hall, ready to take her back to our quarters, but that was too far away. I needed her now. On the left, there was a door and I swiped my hand so it opened.

It was some kind of maintenance room, the space filled entirely with electronics and wires that calibrated the environmental settings of this building. There wasn't much room, but there was a bare wall, a smooth gray one that would not hurt my mate's delicate skin as I reminded her just who she belonged to.

Perfect.

Entering, I pressed the mechanism to lock the door closed behind us so we would not be interrupted, lowered Kristin to her feet.

"What the hell are you doing?" she asked, breathing hard. I hadn't taken her far, so she couldn't be tired, especially since I'd carried her.

"Fucking you." I pushed her up against the wall, but she was so much smaller, she barely reached my shoulder. Easily, I hoisted her up, then leaned into her, pinning her in place with my body. There was no doubt the flare of her eyes was because she felt my cock, long and thick, against her belly, felt my need for her through the collar and her haze of anger and frustration.

The way her breasts rose and fell beneath her blue tunic, she was aroused by our argument, by my touch, by my desire pouring into her mind through the collar.

I was so far gone I wanted to come all over her clothing and then go again, filling her with my seed until she didn't want to argue anymore. The current running between us was magnetic and powerful, pulling us both into a deep, dark well where there would be no escaping.

I felt it and I knew she did as well.

Fuck, I couldn't remember being this hard. Perhaps it was because I felt her wrath, her frustration and her lust through the collar, just as she had mine. The full circle of emotion only built and built until neither of us could argue any further. We had to have a release of all the tension between us and I knew just how to do it.

"Tyran—"

I cut off all argument with a kiss. Wasn't it obvious the reason I'd dragged her away from the others? Hunt had been there when she woke up. When I'd joined them, I'd sensed a calmness between them, which was good, for it was a stark contrast to my dark need for her.

It was so dark I'd had to walk away after we'd claimed her in the transport room. But I couldn't walk away now.

I'd held myself in check, hiding my true nature. But that could not happen any longer. There were no secrets between mates, especially ones who shared collars. Hers was still black, but I sensed her just the same, just as she sensed me.

I took her mouth over and over until her hands lifted to my head, her fingers tunneling into my hair, holding me closer, scraping me with her nails. She tore her mouth from mine, so I kissed her jaw, her cheek, anything I could reach.

"Tyran. We can't do this now. We have men to find," she breathed.

I shook my head slowly and pushed forward, grinding my cock into her soft body as I nibbled on her ear. "*We* don't have to find anything. Hunt does. He's doing his job."

"What's your job?" she asked.

"To keep you safe, at all costs." My words made her groan and I knew she liked the way I felt about her, possessive, protective, a little out of control. I found the base of her neck, her pulse, and bit gently, my reward her bucking hips and a loud moan.

"I need a job. I need something to do or I'll go crazy."

"Not today. Not hunting Hive."

"Today, I could save your men!"

"Today you could get hurt, or die. Not happening, mate."

"So you're just going to fuck me into submission, is that it?"

I gave a slight shrug, lifted my hand and cupped her breast. It was soft and full in my big palm. I felt the nipple tighten and wished her tunic wasn't in the way. "If that's what it takes."

"Why? Why would you want to fuck me? You don't talk to me. It's like we hate each other," she said. Her eyes held the bright flame of anger, but now it was banked with lust. Her hands went to my shirt and I was grateful that I'd listened to Hunt's suggestion. Normally, I wore Coalition armor every day, whether I was on duty or not. But Hunt thought our mate might take advantage of easier access to our bodies, and thank the gods, he'd been right.

Nothing felt better than Kristin's urgent little hands pushing my shirt up so that it came free and bunched between us.

If she hated me, it did not diminish her libido. She was trying to get me naked even as she argued with me.

"No, we're both hot headed." I leaned in and grabbed the collar of her shirt and pulled it to the side, exposing her bare shoulder. I kissed the warm skin, then nipped it. She gasped and her head thumped against the wall. Yes, I loved the taste of her, her scent. "It seems you had an important role on Earth that must carry over here on The Colony."

Her rough hands were able to get under my shirt, at least in the front, and she lifted the fabric up to my armpits. I leaned back enough to yank it over my head. My hips held her firmly in place as I did so. If she wanted my clothes off, I was more than happy to comply. I was in control though and she knew it.

"Yes, but I won't tolerate a jealous mate who won't let me near any other males." She leaned in, found my nipple and took it in her mouth. Then she bit it.

I growled, instantly inflamed and aroused by her bold move. That fucking hurt, but it also made my cock as hard as Prillon ore.

I stepped back, slid her down the wall so her feet touched the floor. I dropped to my knees before her, working her pants off without a bit of finesse.

"You're mine," I said, my words a harsh bark. "Hunt's, too. No other man will touch you."

That wasn't just words. It was a vow and I knew she felt the pulse of it through the collar.

Her pants bunched about her ankles and I worked them free of one foot, but that was all. I didn't need to put any more work in, for I was able to do exactly what I wanted. I pushed her feet apart, wide, then wider still so her pussy was open to me. I cupped that hot, wet flesh in my palm. She cried out at the contact. "This is mine."

"Yes," she hissed, curling her hips outward so she rubbed herself on me.

"You are not officially claimed, not yet. Until you are, I will be possessive." She was wet for me, my fingers instantly slick with her hot need. I moved them back and forth, stroking her, inciting her for more. For me. No one else. *Me.* "Protective and irrational. Nothing but the strength of your mates prevents another male here from claiming you for himself. Most operate on a strict code of honor, and would not tear the collar from your neck. That collar indicates that you belong to me and Hunt, yet it is an outward sign only, and it is still black, a temporary claim, not my family's blue. One tug on it from you or an overeager fighter and I will have to kill to keep you safe."

She stilled, even as I continued to play with her pussy, the scent of her arousal like a drug that calmed my fears for her safety, but stoked another fire within me, one that burned even hotter.

"I thought you said the collars would keep me safe."

I looked up at her, my position one I would only ever assume when I was taking her like this, worshiping her with my body, giving her pleasure. "They are a warning that you are mine, that you have been mated, protected. But the black indicates you are not claimed. I will keep you safe. Yet I will not let another take you away from us, to claim you himself. The testing matched us." I pounded my chest with my free hand. "You're mine, Kristin, whether or not you want to admit it."

She grinned at that. "You *are* jealous."

I slid two fingers into her, deep. Her wet pussy stretched around then before clenching down. She moaned.

"Fuck, of course I am. Every warrior on the planet wants *this*." I worked her, fucking her with my fingers as I would soon be filling her with my cock.

"Tell me what you're going to do to me. How...how you want to claim me," she said, the words barely escaping. She was writhing on my hand, close to coming. Her cheeks were flushed, her thighs quivered, and she wanted me to talk to her, fill her mind with sensual images, tell her what Hunt and I were going to do to her.

The thought sent a jolt of lust up and down my spine before coming to rest in my balls like an iron weight. By the gods, my mate was sex personified, so powerfully feminine, so hot that I feared if she ever learned her true power, I'd be helpless against her.

"My cock will be here." I slid my fingers deeply into her, curling them and pressing against that little ridge of flesh I knew would set her off. She moaned when I took them out. I moved them back to her puckered hole. With her juices coating my fingers, I was able to press and slide one finger into her. The ring of muscle fought my advances, but only briefly, her body relenting and flowering open, allowing me to slip in to the first knuckle.

She gasped, arched her back.

"And Hunt will be here."

I pulled back, worked the second finger into her, then began to slowly, carefully finger fuck her ass. She wasn't a novice at this, knew how to relax, to push out to let me in. She was not afraid of the intense feelings, the intimacy of the act. I watched her face, the way she bit her lip, the way her cheeks turned a pretty pink, the way her breath came out in little pants. I even felt her pussy dripping onto my palm. I didn't need those outward signs to know she liked what I was doing. I felt it through the damn collar. And so I pushed her more. I wanted to see how far she'd go, for I knew how far I wanted to take her. As my matched mate, she'd want it.

No, she'd love it.

"We will fuck you together, fill you with our seed. Don't you see? You will join us as one, just as we've always been meant to be."

She writhed on my fingers. I didn't have enough lube to take her more aggressively, but I would give her what we both needed. I wouldn't relent. Not when she was about to come.

Unable to resist another moment, I leaned forward and tasted her, ran my tongue along the sensitive side of her clit over and over until her legs began to shake. I pushed her to the edge of release, then stopped, again and again until she sobbed once, losing control. Ready to beg.

"That makes you hot, doesn't it? The idea of being fucked by both your men? Your holes stretched, filled, claimed, marked?"

She was panting now, her hands on my shoulders, her fingers digging into my bare skin. "Yes."

"You want to come, don't you?"

"Yes," she repeated.

I stilled my fingers, then pulled them free only long enough to stand, spin her about so her hands were flat on the wall by her head. I lifted the tunic up over her hips, hooked an arm about her to pull her back so she was bent, her pussy and ass on perfect display.

"Don't move," I said as I worked my pants open. Once I

was free, I groaned, the ache in my cock dissipating slightly at the lack of confinement. But seeing her pink and slick, swollen and open for me, I wasn't going to last.

I slid my thumb into her pussy, coated it with her juices and moved it right to her ass, pressing it into the prepared hole, hooking it so it slid in, my palm flat on her luscious ass.

She yelped at the intrusion, but writhed. I didn't delay. I couldn't.

"You want to investigate the missing men? You want to be out of my sight?"

Lining up, I thrust into her pussy. She cried out, her arms bending so her forearms were on the wall, her cheek pressed against the hard surface.

I had to bend my knees to get into her, but once I was buried to the balls, I wrapped my free arm around her waist and settled my palm over her clit, lifted her, pulled her up and back onto my cock as my fingers toyed with her sensitive nub. "Spread your legs, mate. I want you wide open as I fuck you."

"Oh, God." Her pussy fluttered around my hard length and I froze in place, waited for the moment to pass. Her hands tightened into fists against the wall and she moaned my name.

I could listen to that sweet sound for hours.

Moving slowly, I told her how I felt as I fucked her. "You're mine. Mine. Do you understand? Your pussy is mine. Your heart is mine. You will not want a new mate. You will not look at the other warriors. You will love me, do you understand?"

I felt like a primitive idiot babbling as I thrust into her, but the hot, wet heat of her was making me lose my mind.

The words were rough and unfiltered, dragged from the deepest, darkest places inside, but I couldn't hold them back. Not with her.

She made me lose control. She brought out the darkness. I only hoped she could accept it, because the monster that was my dark side, my buried needs and desires, had escaped his prison locked inside my soul and no matter how hard I tried to go back to the way I was before, I couldn't. She'd broken me open and spilled my soul into the world, into her. I couldn't put it back.

My hips rammed home, pressing against the back of my hand, driving my thumb into her with each thrust. She would have a small taste of what it would feel like with both of us taking her, fucking her, filling her up.

"I am not kind. I am jealous, possessive." She came with a wail and I didn't stop, just fucked her harder, sweat dripping down my brow, my balls drawing up, my orgasm building at the base of my spine. "Obsessed."

"Tyran," she wailed, her walls already milking my cock.

I didn't relent, giving her exactly what she needed as she came again, harder, her pussy going into spasms around my shaft. I gritted my teeth, the feel of her tight heat around my cock my own personal heaven. And hell. There would be no escaping her. No denying her. She would own me.

Fuck. She already did.

Her pleasure triggered my release. Her screams, no doubt, could be heard through this entire section of the base, but I didn't care. I wanted everyone to know that I was her mate, that I was giving her what she needed, and that she was well taken care of.

I didn't want any of these bastards to think they could do better.

She would live here, work here, make friends and talk to people, but I'd be the one she came home to. Hunt would be waiting with me. We'd be the ones to strip her bare and take her, fuck her. Fill her. Love her.

Make her scream.

My orgasm hit and I staggered forward, for a short time vulnerable. I couldn't protect her when my pleasure took over. I couldn't do anything except close my eyes and give over as I came, lost to the bliss only to be found in my mate. My cock thickened inside her, thrust deep and bottomed out, pulsed with the need to expel my seed, to fill her. I did, coating her walls, filling her womb. I groaned, leaned forward and slapped my hand on the wall. The sound of the metal denting echoed in the small room.

Only after I caught my breath did I lower her to the ground and drop to kneel behind her. The movement had my cock slipping free. Carefully, I slid my thumb from her, watched her as she caught her breath. She hadn't moved, but her eyes were closed and I felt a sense of lethargy, euphoria and satisfaction coming from her.

I grunted at the sight of my seed slipping from her, coating her thighs, a bold drop slipping to the floor between my knees. I got hard at the sight of my claim, knowing I'd filled her.

"You're mine, Kristin. Never forget who you belong to."

She turned then, dropped to my lap and cupped my face with her hands.

"I won't forget."

"Me and Hunt. No one else touches you."

"You're such a caveman."

Her bold answer made me grin. "You're mine. Say it."

She shook her head and bit her full lower lip, just hard enough to make me want to taste it and I groaned.

Her eyes darkened and she studied my face. I wondered what she saw there. My features were not human, my nose and cheeks too angular, my coloring different, my teeth longer and sharper than the men from her world. She studied me like I was a complex puzzle, and leaned forward to place a soft, tender kiss on my lips. I'd never been kissed like that, the gentleness made me shiver, an unfamiliar ache settling deep in my chest. "I am beginning to believe, Captain, that you have that backwards."

"How so?"

"I'm pretty sure you two belong to me."

She was right. So fucking right. This woman owned me, but I wasn't going to admit it to her. Not now. Maybe not ever.

ristin

I PACED the confines of our quarters, fuming. I had no idea if my irritation could reach my mates through the collar, but I couldn't make myself care. I was no eight-year-old little princess running around in sparkly shoes needing my big, strong daddies to protect me.

For three days, my mates had kept me here, locked away for my own safety while they'd been out there hunting for the missing men and coming away empty handed. Three days! I'd managed to get my hands on one of the ion blasters, but they'd found it—damn the collars for the sense of satisfaction I'd felt at grabbing the stupid thing—and promptly taken it away from me like I was a helpless child, not a trained Federal Agent.

I told them about my job, my skills, my experience, but they didn't care. Earth was a lesser planet to them, which made my abilities *lesser*. I knew they saw me as an equal. No, they placed my life above theirs. I knew they valued me, well, I felt that. But it wasn't my value or equality on the table here, it was my skills. My abilities.

They would give me anything I wanted...except when it came to my protection. They wouldn't care if I had Wonder Woman bracelets that deflected bullets, they weren't putting me in harm's way. I didn't want to go into danger, but I was completely useless here, trapped and feeling helpless. Neither condition I tolerated well.

I kept telling myself that they didn't know me, didn't truly know or understand what I was capable of, but that wasn't enough to satisfy the discontent growing inside me like a cancer. The missing warriors were still MIA, even my powerful Prillon mates and the other twenty Colony warriors out searching every day couldn't find them. Every evening, my mates came back from their fruitless search and fucked me until I couldn't breathe before falling into an exhausted sleep.

They had granted me access to Base 3's reports database, thanks to my anger, and at both Governor Rone's and Rachel's insistence. My mates had no problem allowing me to read and analyze data that might assist them in their search. From afar. But they would not let me go out and actually interview anyone, look in their eyes, watch for lies, ticks, nerves. Reports were great, but nothing was better than staring someone down and making them squirm. Seeing the truth even when they spouted lies.

I'd been the princess locked in the tower long enough. And I was done waiting.

Walking to the communications panel next to the door of our quarters, I waved my hand over it, pushed it, stared at it, trying to make it work. Something must have triggered, because I got a response from one of the communications officers somewhere on Base 3. His face appeared on the small screen and I squinted to get a better look. He wasn't Prillon, looked far too human for that. Deep green eyes, caramel colored skin, and wavy hair that was the color of melted brown sugar.

He was gorgeous. Stunning. And to my absolute disgust, I found him utterly and completely unattractive. He could win modeling contests back on Earth, and for all the interest I had, I might as well have been talking to a block of Swiss cheese.

Boring, boring man. No heat. No fire. Not enough badass alien for my newly acquired tastes. Tyran and Hunt had ruined me for all others. I wanted what I wanted and that was my mates. And they were mine. The overprotective jerks. So, if my pussy was telling me I was stuck with them, they were going to have to learn to behave.

"Lady Zakar, how may I assist?"

"What planet are you from?" I blurted the question without thinking, but then, that's what I did. I asked questions. It was kind of my specialty.

"Trion, my lady. Do you require assistance?"

"Yes. Get these two monster sized guards out of my hair." While I couldn't see them through the closed door, I knew they were there. The two Prillon warriors standing guard were meant to keep me safe. Which was a joke. Give me freaking gun and I'd take care of that myself.

At his confused look, I gave up on the slang and said something even a hard-headed, alpha male alien would understand.

"I need to speak to Lady Rone immediately. Please ask her to come to my quarters at once."

"Yes, my lady." He nodded and disappeared from the screen. I knew he'd do what I asked. No doubt, Rachel would arrive with a string of her own guards, which might present a problem. But I would deal with one challenge at a time.

The fury growing inside me was shocking, but it shouldn't have been. I'd dedicated my life on Earth to protecting people, to tracking down criminals and seeing justice done. That these wounded Colony warriors wouldn't allow me to help made me feel like I had cockroaches crawling around inside my chest. The feeling made me crazed, made me want to hiss and scream and throw things in the mother of all meltdowns.

But that wasn't my style. I'd learned how to cage my rage and helplessness, strap it down deep in my mind and function, despite the emotions clogging my throat. The horribleness of what I'd seen, what I'd uncovered in all my years with the FBI would have put me in the looney bin otherwise. But for the first time in years I struggled to maintain control. And why?

I knew why, because my mates, the men I was growing to love, the men I'd given myself to, surrendered to, were now the ones holding me back.

As much as I needed Tyran's strong handed dominance in the bedroom, I wasn't willing to give up that level of control in other areas of my life. Hunt, I was sure, would come around eventually. I would need to make him understand and then ask him to help me handle Tyran.

As much as that caveman male could be *handled.*

In their arms, in their bed, I could let go, give up my iron control and be free in a way I never was anywhere else. I craved those moments, that release.

But this was something else entirely. This was evil stalking the citizens of my new home, and The Colony— and every warrior here—was mine now. This was my new family, which meant these people were mine. Just like the girls I'd helped save on Earth were mine. It wasn't logical, but serving the community wasn't about logic. Neither was being with two hard-headed warriors even though they were a pain in my ass.

I'd watched a movie once where a father explained things to his little boy by grouping all people into one of three types: sheep, wolves, or sheepdogs.

Protecting the people—the sheep—from the wolves was just what I did. And as shocked as I was by the fact that I was on an alien world, with aliens for husbands, that one fundamental truth about me hadn't changed. Not. One. Bit. I was not prey.

Yet, it seemed my mates thought of me as a sheep. Until they saw me for what I was, the ruthless, relentless guard dog, then we'd have problems and I'd be pissed.

A chime of some sort sounded and I jumped, startled out of my thoughts. Must be the doorbell. Who knew there were space doorbells?

I walked to the door and waved my hand over the control panel. Nearly silent, the entry slid sideways, revealing Rachel standing on the other side. She was dressed in the green that I'd learned meant she was part of the medical staff, a doctor. Her dark brown hair was pulled back in a braid and her face was bare of makeup. But her skin practically glowed, and I shoved aside a bit of envy. With her olive colored skin, she looked like a Greek goddess. I should have hated her for being at least three inches taller than me. I'd always felt like a white orchid that just melted or burned to a crisp in the sun. With my blond hair cut in a pixie style, my pale skin nearly translucent, and all the extra junk in the trunk, I felt like an ugly duckling facing a dark swan. I wanted to hate her for all of it, but she was too nice. She forced me to adore her, which just wasn't entirely fair.

Then again, I was used to women prettier than me. But even as the usual self-deprecating thoughts ran through my mind, a formidable, primitive part of me rose up and filled me with confidence and feminine power. Rachel was beautiful and brilliant. A scientist who'd figured out what the Hive had been up to a few months ago, when her mate, Maxim, had become ill and a human named Brooks had died. She's solved the puzzle and saved the lives of everyone on this planet. Not the powerful Prillons, not the Atlan beasts. *Her.*

But Tyran and Hunt didn't want her, they wanted me. I wasn't a scientist, I wasn't tall and dark, but I was theirs. I was strong and relentless. I knew beyond a shadow of a doubt just how violent their feelings for me were, because I could sense everything through the collars. Felt it with every touch. Reveled in it with every orgasm.

They didn't *pretend* to be obsessed with me, to desire me. Their obsession, the intense attraction was real. And that gave me more confidence than ever. I'd never felt stronger, more capable.

Unfortunately for them, it also made me less likely to stay in this room like a good little mate while they went out into the world hunting bad guys without me. No. Fucking. Way.

Rachel lifted her brow as I peeked over her shoulder

into the cream colored corridor. Behind her stood not two, but four additional guards. Two Prillon I didn't know, an Atlan named Rezz and a dark, brooding Everian Hunter I'd met yesterday at dinner. They were all new arrivals on The Colony and Hunt told me he was confident that serving guard duty over the governor's mate would be a good way to make them feel included and part of the community without giving them too much opportunity to cause trouble. One of the missing men, Lieutenant Perro, had been their friend.

Hunt wanted to keep an extra close eye on them. Guess he'd succeeded. Especially since they were working with other, long-time Colony residents.

The assignment to protect me or Rachel must have felt like traffic duty for city cops as far as I was concerned. Boring as hell. If I was safe inside our quarters, there wasn't too much danger right outside the doorway. I actually felt bad for the two Prillon standing guard. Captain Marz was new to The Colony, and one of my personal shadows anytime Hunt and Tyran had to go to work. If I got to leave our rooms.

If my mates were protective, Governor Rone and Captain Ryston were, evidently, twice as bad. Four guards? Cue the eye-roll. Seriously.

"Hi, Kristin. Are you all right?" Rachel's words were in English, and I grinned. The NPU worked wonders, translating the various languages spoken on The Colony almost instantly, but it was still nice to hear someone from home.

"Hi. I'm fine. Just mad. Can we talk?"

She nodded over her shoulder before stepping inside

my quarters, the door sliding closed behind her so we could speak alone. I sighed.

"And now there are six huge-ass warriors wasting their time standing outside my room."

Rachel laughed, her brown eyes sparkling, which helped cool some of my temper. If anyone knew what hell I was going through at the moment, it had to be her. "They do tend to be a little over-protective."

I wasn't one to mince words, not when it came to work. "I need armor and a gun."

The humor in her gaze faded quickly and she studied me with a somber expression. "Are you sure that's a good idea?"

"Has anything like this—the missing warriors—happened on The Colony before? How many of these guys are skilled investigators? I know they all fought in the war, but killing bad guys and talking to them are two very different skill sets."

She paced from the door to the tiny table in the makeshift eating area. The place was set up like an efficiency apartment back on Earth, a barely-there kitchen —because most times the warriors ate together in the community dining halls—two couches and the S-Gen unit in the corner. There was a chair I could imagine curling up in to read, and a very large bed that I couldn't bear to look at just now. Remembering what my mates had done to me in it would distract me from my plan.

"I know you're right, but these aren't drug dealers or pimps, Kristin. And this isn't Earth. They're Hive."

I shook my head. I knew enough. "I've been reading about them. Reading the reports. I've pored through hundreds, maybe thousands of documents in the database over the last few days. I know what I'm getting into. They're trying to re-assimilate everyone on this planet, to take it over, and I'm not going to let them have my mates, or anyone else."

"What?" Rachel's dark brows winged up and she stopped cold. "What did you just say?"

I crossed my arms over my chest, my dark blue tunic and pants annoying to me now when I wanted to be wearing armor like my mates.

I sighed. "Come on, Rachel. Are you trying to tell me that's not exactly what you think is going on here?"

She shook her head and took a couple steps closer to me, her voice slow, each word drawn out as if she was thinking about them even as they left her mouth. "No...but how could you possibly know that? We haven't told the rest of the citizens on The Colony for fear it would start a panic. How did you find out?"

Tilting my head to the side, I raised one brow and knew the skepticism showed on my face. "Really? It's all there, in the reports. You just have to read between the lines."

"Shit." Rachel laughed. "You are good."

I grinned and it felt fabulous that my assumptions had been validated. "It's what I do."

"Yes, you're right. Fine." She sighed. "I'm going to get in trouble for this, but all right. I'm in. If we're going to be BFFs, we might as well start raising hell and breaking them in. I'd been doing it all by myself up until now. It'll be better with a partner-in-crime. What do you want to do?"

I hugged her. Hard. I couldn't help it. "BFFs," I agreed.

She grinned, hugging me back, her face full of mischief. "Okay, Miss FBI. What kind of trouble are we going to get into today?"

I let her go and paced in front of her, gathering my thoughts. "I read your medical reports. I read about the death of Captain Brooks and about the man you think was responsible, the Prillon medical officer who disappeared. Krael?"

Rachel's expression said more than words. Hate was strange to see on her normally kind face. "Yes. That's his name. He murdered Brooks and nearly killed Maxim and then disappeared, crawled back into a hole like the rat he is. Others would have died if we hadn't figured out what he'd been up to."

"I don't think the fact that Krael was never caught, and that now, three months later, warriors are disappearing is just a coincidence. Did he have friends? Family? Who did he train with? Eat with? Sleep with? Work with?"

"He worked in medical with Doctor Surnen. I can vouch for the doc. He's arrogant, but he's no traitor. He nearly worked himself to death trying to figure out what was going on with Maxim. At first he was a misogynistic jerk, but he's grown on me and I think I may have changed his perspective on some things. As for the rest of your questions, I don't know, but we can find out."

"Yes, we can." Our gazes locked and I knew she was all-in. "But first I need armor, and a gun."

Rachel told me to strip and led me to the S-Gen pad where she ordered armor and then helped me get into it. I looked good, and the armor was surprisingly lightweight and flexible. Formfitting and maneuverable. Rachel gave me a critical once-over and nodded. "Good. The armor will deflect basic ion blasts, but that's all I know about it."

I pulled the small, silver ion blaster from its holster on my thigh and felt my face practically crack in half, my smile was so big. It felt good to hold a weapon again, to know it was to help track down a bad guy and end him. "Do you know how to fire this thing?"

She shook her head. "I'm a lab nerd. Sorry."

With a shrug, I turned, pointed at the reading chair and fired. An explosion of sound accompanied the chair bursting into flames, the fluffy guts that I'd once sat upon floating through the air like glowing cinders from a wood fire riding a breeze.

"Excellent."

ristin

IT WAS EVEN BETTER than my Glock 23. Lighter, a smoother trigger, less kick. Way more powerful. I could get used to having it.

"Woman, you are bat-shit crazy." Rachel chuckled as the door slid open and all six guards rushed into the room with their own weapons drawn and aimed at the now smoking chair.

I ignored them, looking up into her laughing eyes. "Does that mean we can't be besties?"

"Hell no. I like you even better now that you shot the shit out of your chair."

I laughed, completely happy for the first time in days. Freedom sang through my veins like the sweetest poison. I knew I was going to have to face down my mates over this, but I was tired of sitting around like a bump on a log. I'd talked and talked about it, but while they heard me, they hadn't listened. If I was going to make a go of our match, then I had to be myself. If I allowed them to keep me locked up and safe, then I'd be spending the rest of my life in this damn room. And if Tyran wanted to spank me later...well, it would be worth it. And, I wasn't completely opposed to that since I liked it every time he'd done it so far. "Good. Let's go."

We headed for the door but Captain Marz stepped in front of me. I knew he was new to The Colony from what my mates had told me. Him and the dark eyed Everian Hunter next to him. They were shoulder to shoulder, their features nothing alike—Marz was Prillon and the other looked like a human, just bigger...a lot bigger. Both of them frowned at me, but it was the Captain who spoke. "What do you believe you are doing, Lady Zakar?"

I lifted a brow. "I'm going to go shake down a few people, find out what's going on around here. Find our missing warriors." I made a show of putting the blaster back in its holster on my thigh before lifting my head to look up at them both again. Way up. The Hunter, Kiel was his name, was trying to hide a grin, and failing. The Captain, however, was far from amused. I didn't look behind them at the other men. Hell, I couldn't see around them, they were too dang big. The Atlan in the back was beyond huge, but I knew Marz was in charge by the way the others let him do all the talking. He was the one I needed to convince, so I looked at him.

"I don't think your mates would approve," he said.

"I don't need their permission." I crossed my arms as Rachel came to stand behind me. "I *do* need your help." That was the truth. I needed all the manpower I could get and I assumed alien power would be even better. "You can either stay here, bored out of your minds watching my door, or you can come along, protect me and Lady Rone, and maybe do a little hunting of your own. One of your men is missing, too. Lieutenant Perro?"

I had him. I knew it when his eyes narrowed and he took a deep, deep breath, the kind you take when you're about to say something you know you shouldn't. "Lead the way."

Rachel looked at me. "Where do you want to start?"

"Krael's personal quarters."

She nodded. "I know where he was staying."

Rachel nodded to Captain Marz as she passed and the other warriors fell into step behind her. The three who weren't part of Marz's group looked like they were about to argue, but Warlord Rezzer crossed his arms and said one word.

"Move."

The unknown Prillon closest to the Atlan opened his mouth, closed it, looked at Captain Marz, who was already waving them away.

"Two of you stay here and make sure no one gets into Lady Zakar's rooms. You," he pointed to the third, "Go back to command and tell the governor where we're headed."

"Yes, sir."

After that, everyone fell into line and I followed Rachel through about a quarter mile of corridors and covered walkways. The entire base was enclosed due to severe lightning storms that struck, sometimes with little to no warning. I hadn't seen much yet, except the inside of my room, and I was eager to explore.

Beyond the corridors, outside the Base, I saw endless rocky landscapes and ravines dotted by buildings in a circular grid. I knew from my reading that there were vertical housing units, training facilities, but mostly mining. There was an element on this planet I'd never heard of. Apparently, it was rare, so unstable they couldn't use their S-Gen technology to create it, and absolutely necessary for the operation of their transport stations.

Which made me angry. They'd taken their wounded veterans, those who carried Hive technology, the survivors, and sent them to this Colony planet to be miners?

Really? That was the best they could come up with? Hunt explained to me that there were seven bases on the planet, and three of them were completely underground.

Like any bride from Earth was going to want wind up *there.* Not that I spoke the thought aloud. I didn't need to. My mates had felt my dislike for that idea through the collars. Then again, maybe it was just me. There could be a spelunker from back home who wouldn't mind living like a bat in a cave. But that *she* was not me.

Rachel knew her way around and we were before a closed door just a few minutes later. Krael's quarters. The Hunter, Kiel, moved to the front and stood before it. He took several deep breaths, moving his head around the edges and the control panel as if he was some kind of bloodhound.

The process was both fascinating and weird and drove home the fact that I wasn't on Earth anymore, that these guys were *all* aliens.

"Your mates have been here," Kiel opened his eyes and stared down at me like I'd have some kind of explanation.

I shrugged. "That's not surprising, considering they've been looking for the missing men."

Kiel shook his head and looked over my shoulder,

sharing a look with Captain Marz, who stood behind me like a towering oak. "What is it?" Marz asked.

"They were not alone."

Cold jelly fingers wrapped around my heart from the inside and I fought to remain still. "Tell me. I can see it in your eyes that something's wrong." I glared at the Hunter, daring him to lie. "Tell me."

Kiel didn't look at Marz again, which won him brownie points with me just as Warlord Rezzer growled and took a step closer to Rachel. Distracted, I turned to look at the Atlan and saw the bones in his face appear to shift under his skin. His shoulders bulked up, but just when I thought I was going to get to see my first Atlan beast, he stopped changing, stuck in some kind of half-way in between. The one word he spoke, however, killed every ounce of curiosity I had.

"Hive."

Kiel nodded when I turned back to him.

"Hive? Here?"

The half-beast growled again, the sound almost loud enough to drown out the pounding of my pulse inside my ears.

Kiel leaned into the door and took another slow, measured breath. "Yes. True Hive. An Integration Unit and at least two Soldiers." His eyes darkened, looking resigned. "And Perro. I scent the missing Prillon. He has been here, too."

Scent? I had absolutely no idea how he knew this by just staring at a door and the entry control panel, but I was impressed. This Everian's nose was almost as good as a German Shepherd's. I was not happy about his findings, but definitely impressed.

"By the gods." Marz pulled his gun free and I followed

suit, my adrenaline pumping. This hunt was on full-throttle now. "Were they with Hunt and Tyran?"

With a nod, Kiel activated his comm device and spoke to someone in Base 3 command. "What is the current location of Captains Treval and Zakar?"

There was a long pause on the other end, but eventually the Prillon warrior that Marz had sent back to base answered. I had a thing for voices, and I recognized his. "They are several hours overdue. There are two search teams out looking for them now."

What?

A scream built in my throat, but I didn't let it out. I didn't want to scare these big, bad aliens with a screech that would surely make their ears bleed. "My mates are *missing*, and no one bothered to *tell me?*"

Rachel stepped up next to me and put her hand on my arm. I didn't want to be touched, but I held still, forced myself to behave. "We'll find them."

Kiel thanked the officer and turned away from the door, walking off in a direction that looked like it went...well, absolutely nowhere.

"Where are you going?" I asked.

"Your mates were taken this way. Do you want to go with me now, or stay here and wait to summon assistance?"

Forget waiting. My mates were missing and Kiel knew which way they went? Yeah, no decision making needed. "Let's go." I hurried to catch up, Warlord Rezzer and Captain Marz falling in step behind me. Rachel, however, hung back. I glanced over my shoulder. "What's up?"

She tilted her head and put her hands on her hips. "I'm going to go back and get some help. We'll be right behind you."

I nodded and looked down as I took my first steps off the manufactured walkways of the Base and onto hard red rock. A few random shrubs struggled to survive in the rocky terrain and suddenly I didn't feel like I was home at all. I felt like I was on Mars, and the two most important people on the planet were out there lost in the maze of rock and caves. No, not lost. Taken. They needed me.

I'd only been loved, really loved, by my mates for a few days but that was long enough for me to know I wasn't willing to give that up. I was addicted, and I was going to get them back.

Tyran, Hive Containment Cell, The Colony

I woke to the sound of boots approaching, the sound traveling through the stone beneath me to rumble up into my ears. Whoever was coming was big, heavy, and an enemy. Next to me on the cold stone floor of our cell, Hunt blinked slowly, the reality of our situation jolting him awake.

We heard shouts, a fight, feet sliding over the hard floor. An ion blast. They were taking whoever was in the cell next to ours. They were going to torture him, integrate him. Make him fully Hive.

Anger roiled through me, but I had no outlet. We couldn't save whoever it was. There was nothing we could do but hope they destroyed him quickly.

"They'll be coming for us. Not right now, but soon."

Yes, they would be busy for a little while.

"Fuck," I breathed. "I know." I twisted my fingers, popping the broken bones back into proper alignment so I could use them again. Pain wouldn't stop me. No doubt Doctor Surnen would give me a hard time about it, but if we made it out of here alive, I was more than willing to take that verbal attack.

"We have to get out of here before any more get dragged away. Warn the others." Hunt rolled his head around on his neck, stretching, waking up, getting ready to fight. "At least one of us," he said, his words uttered through a clenched jaw.

I knew that, too. The warriors sent to The Colony had been made a promise, a promise that they would never again have to fear Hive Integration. That for them, the war was over. That they were safe.

Which was a lie. The Hive Soldiers who ambushed us had been on Base 3, walking the perimeter of Section 9 like they belonged there. No alarms went off, no guards yelled a warning. We'd even approached them with a casualness of new acquaintances, as fellow members of the community, not as the enemy. They circled and we'd been unprepared, weapons still in their holsters. Ambushed. Taken.

No wonder so many men were missing. There had been no warning. No gun fight. No battle. Nothing but surprise. And we'd fallen for it, too.

Fuck. The Hive shouldn't be able to destroy us. We'd thought ourselves beyond all that. The Colony was a far-flung planet with very little to offer a conquering horde. We had no need to lock doors or fear attack. We were deep in Coalition space. We should have been safe.

We weren't.

Down here in this pseudo prison, we'd discovered the

truth about our missing warriors. They were gone, either dead or fully integrated into the Hive's control system. Even now, Lieutenant Perro paced in front of our prison cell, no expression in his eyes. The man he used to be was gone. Depending on how one wanted to look at it, the others, the dead men lining the halls, got off easier. At least they were free. Their suffering was over. They hadn't been turned into the enemy, into everything we'd fought against.

We were honorable and being turned into the Hive was the cruelest of fates. Death was better.

We hadn't been integrated yet as the other missing men had, but our time would come. The cut on Hunt's head oozed and he wobbled a bit as he tried to sit up. No doubt he had a concussion. The way he was moving his arm, rotating it around, testing it, I figured he probably dislocated the joint. He'd done it once before, in a battle in Sector 17. They'd put him in the regeneration pod after for it to heal, but he still rubbed it once in a while, as if chasing a phantom ache.

I'd fared better today. I only had three broken fingers and a few broken ribs. I'd had worse. Much worse. I could still fight. Soon, that would be the only thing that mattered.

Our wounds were all easily healed by a ReGen wand, which we didn't have.

They'd stripped us of everything. Ion pistols, comm units, healers. We still wore our armor, but otherwise we'd be naked. I wasn't modest. I didn't give a shit if the Hive and the traitors saw my naked ass. But I was grateful we still had our armor. From past experience I knew that once the armor was removed, the real pain began.

"This is wrong." Hunt leaned his back against the wall

with a sigh, and using the cold stone to steady him, he closed his eyes. "I refuse to believe fate would be so cruel."

I knew, without asking I knew he was talking about our mate. We'd just found her, tasted her, made her ours. We'd just begun to heal and become whole again.

I sighed and leaned back next to him, shoulder to shoulder as we'd faced everything the last few years. "Maybe she was a final gift." I'd been thinking about our mate, beyond grateful that she'd been mine, even if it was only for a short time. I didn't care about anything but Kristin's safety, her care. If we died, another would care for her. She was beautiful and perfect, impossible not to love. And thank fuck, she wasn't here.

She was safe at Base 3 with the governor, his slew of guards, with the others.

The truth would come out eventually. I had confidence in our fellow warriors. They would discover this place and destroy it, although I wasn't sure if it would happen before or after they tried to integrate us into the Hive.

Back and forth I watched our lone guard pace. Lieutenant Perro had been completely turned into a Hive Soldier. While he looked somewhat like himself—physique, hair color, appearance, that was it. He was a machine, a warrior, but with full Hive frequencies rattling around in his head until there was nothing else left. His brain was gone. He was no longer Perro.

He'd survived the ruthless torture of the Hive once, but to have suffered through it again knowing he wouldn't escape? That wasn't just torture, it was madness. "I won't let them remake me into the enemy. They'll have to kill me."

13

 yran

HUNT SNARLED AT MY WORDS. "Shut up. We're going to be smart about this. They don't know how strong you are, what was done to you. We'll get out of here, and then we'll kill the traitor."

"How could we not know about Krael, about his treachery?" That's what I wanted to know. He'd lived among us, worked among us. He had friends. Why had he turned? And turned he had indeed. He was acting of his own free will, not controlled internally and automatically by the Hive menace. I'd seen the bastard walking around, giving orders.

I wanted to kill him. But first, we had to get out of this cell. And to do that, we had to either figure out how to walk through solid rock, or discover a way to get around the force field trapping us here. I'd stopped trying to find ways past the shimmering energy field blocking the front of our rock cell, that energy the sole barrier keeping us imprisoned for the past few hours. Had it been hours? Days? How long had we slept?

Deep in the cave, there was no sense of time. Nothing for us to gauge how long we'd been held, how long until they would come for us. How long it would be until our transformations were complete. They'd started on us once before, but we'd escaped. Soon they'd finish us.

I'd tried to get out. Yeah, there was no fucking way to escape. Thick rock on three sides with the fourth deceivingly open. It was like the Atlan cells, with an impenetrable field of energy even an Atlan beast couldn't break through. It wasn't about strength, but science. I knew what happened when touching it; I was lucky only my fingers were broken. I could have lost a hand if I'd pressed against the invisible field too hard.

"It was our jobs to know," Hunt replied.

I turned my head, looked at my friend, my fellow warrior, my fellow mate. "There was no way we could have known. We trusted one another too much. Without Lady Rone, we might never have discovered the deception. Maxim didn't know. He's the governor and still had no idea. Unless you are implying he was in on it?"

Why was I the practical one in this? We hadn't known the depth of Krael's treachery, not until now. No, that was wrong. We knew *someone* was destroying The Colony, one warrior at a time. Preying on them, kidnapping them, converting them and making them into drones, into warriors *for* the Hive.

"Fuck no. I trust Maxim with my life."

"What's done is done. Brooks is dead. And The Colony will be destroyed if we don't stop Krael. Yes, he got away once before, but we knew who to look for. And now he's here. With us. We have to kill him." I didn't keep my voice down, I wanted Perro to hear us, hoped he'd be foolish enough to turn and lower the force field trapping us. He twitched, as if listening, but resumed pacing, ignoring us completely. He was gone.

"Krael is one thing. No one is prepared for this." Hunt waved his hand through the air indicating our current predicament, the secret base. All of it. "I don't know if killing Krael will be enough." This complex, the number of Hive walking around, was much more than we'd expected to find, and much more dangerous to everyone on The Colony.

"I know."

We sat in silence and I welcome the quiet preparing myself for what was to come. I would not succumb to the Hive processing. I would fight to the death, take as many of them with me as I could. Hunt had to escape, warn the others, take care of Kristin.

"I'm going to rip them to pieces, Hunt. When it starts, get the hell out of here. Take care of Kristin. Warn the others. This has to be stopped."

"There is no stopping us." Krael appeared at the front of our rock cell, standing on the other side of the force field, just out of reach. We were on the floor, our backs resting against the cold, unforgiving rock. We'd stood and paced for a long time when we'd first arrived, but knew to conserve our energy for when it was time to fight back. We would have risen if the person facing us warranted respect, but Krael deserved none.

More, we hoped our appearance of cooperation would entice them to lower the force field.

Krael did no such thing, just stared down his pompous

nose at us. "The Colony will be slowly infiltrated by the Hive. We will conquer this world and it will host a complete Hive battlegroup. We will be able to attack the closest member planets with ease from this location. After that, all of you *veterans*—" he spat out Queen Deston's honorific for those that lived on The Colony as if it were foul, "—will be considered ruthless killers and destroyed on sight."

He was right. If The Colony was taken over by the Hive, the general population of all Coalition planets would think all returning warriors were tainted, regardless of whether they'd been integrated and escaped or not. Any hope of recovery from Hive implants and integration would be lost. Hatred and loathing would spread for us, already the most feared members of the interplanetary community. We'd destroy ourselves, be exterminated by our own peoples, and the Hive would ensure the job was complete.

"Not going to happen," Hunt growled, refusing to look up at the traitor.

Krael had the audacity to grin. "Yes, it will. And by you. The two of you will mindlessly work for the Hive in destroying first this planet and the community you've worked so hard to create." The horror that would follow he left unsaid. We all knew what would happen if The Colony fell under the Hive control. Earth was the closest, and least protected, planet. Humanity would fall first. Kirstin's home. Her people.

He was a worthless excuse for a Prillon. While he was as large and forbidding as Hunt and myself, he lacked honor. I had no idea when he'd switched allegiances, but he'd destroyed plenty already. At least what we knew about.

He had no Hive integration that I could see. No new eye like Hunt. No bots in muscle like I had. What had the Hive done to him? Did he have integrations in his arms, torso? Or had they modified his brain? He spoke as himself, sounded cognizant of his choices, and that made me hate him. He wasn't being controlled or manipulated, he betrayed us all for his own selfish ends. What those were, I neither knew nor cared. His motives were irrelevant. He was the enemy. First chance I had, I was going to rip him in half.

The missing men who'd been taken recently were mindless Hive drones now. We'd seen them as we were brought here. While they looked like their former selves, they were a shell, a functioning unit controlled by the Hive. The portion of their brains that made them individuals was gone, disconnected.

But Krael? He wasn't mindless. No, he was too cunning, too ruthless. While he *worked* for the Hive, I had to wonder how he was *controlled* by them.

He worked alone, at least as far as we could tell. It was unusual for a Prillon, most had a second, even if they had no mate, a trusted brother to keep the loneliness at bay. But Krael was a mystery, one we would solve if we could get out of the damn cell. He had no collar, no connection to anyone but the Hive.

He grinned, but the expression was cold.

"Your time is coming. Soon. But I'll leave you here to wonder when." He angled his head toward Lieutenant Perro. "He's been converted so nicely. He used to side with you, protect your back. Now he will shoot you there. At my command or at the Hive's whim. He patted the now Hive controlled warrior on the shoulder, but Lieutenant Perro didn't even blink in response to the action. "With him, we put him under before we inserted the Hive processing unit in his prefrontal cortex. He can't decide to take a piss without permission. But with you?" He shrugged. "We'll see. The fun of what they are doing here is finding different ways to re-integrate. What was done to you before was simple experimentation in comparison."

He studied Hunt's eye, squinting. "They'll finish what they started with you, Hunt. The frontal eye fields will be fully integrated. You'll be walking eyes for the Hive."

Hunt blinked, slowly, but refused to rise to the bait.

My uninjured hand fisted. I wanted to kill Krael with a ferocity I'd never known before. But I contained it, controlled it, like I always did with my emotions. I had to bide my time. There would be a moment of opportunity, I just had to wait for it.

He turned and left then, his footsteps heavy on the rock floor, leaving Lieutenant Perro to remain as our guard, the once proud warrior now our constant reminder of Hive power and ultimately our own weakness.

Hunt pushed to his feet, put a hand on the wall to steady himself. "We have to do something. We can't just stay here, trapped, waiting to die."

I looked up at him. He was used to being in control, as was I. It was in our very cells, to lead, to dominate. Being trapped as we were was doubly hard for us. I was just as angry as Hunt, but I was always the cool headed one. At least in situations like this. In battle, I was ice cold. Precise.

Hunt could lead, was a diplomat and a strategist. But now? Now he was seething with anger and it bubbled over. The darkness he never showed escaping, anger flaring with every glance at Lieutenant Perro.

"Krael will die for this. And slowly."

I didn't say anything. I didn't need to.

After a few minutes of letting Hunt fume, I had to be

analytical. To think clearly, logically and not be driven by the depth of our anger. "We can do nothing now. We must wait for the opportunity. It will come, but we must be ready. We must be strong. Rest. Your head must feel like a fucking boulder."

Hunt turned, sighed. He let his shoulders drop, let the tense angles settle, at least for now. He knew I was right, knew we needed to let it all go, at least for now. "It does. Shit." He moved and dropped back to the floor beside me.

To conserve our strength. To wait.

Tyran, Containment Cell, Hive Caves

I MUST HAVE SLEPT. I had no idea how long, but the sound of boots woke me again. With my elbow, I nudged Hunt, who stirred. "It's time."

Hunt's eyes opened, then when he heard the footsteps, his jaw clenched. He stood slowly, a hand on the wall. Thank fuck for the collars, for I sensed while his head still hurt, it wouldn't be too much. He needed a clear, focused head, not a concussed one. I rose to my feet as well. Waited. Side by side as always.

Perro and a purely evil Hive Integration Unit stood on the other side of the energy field. The Hive moved to press some button and the continuous whirring sound stopped and I knew the energy field was off. My ears rang from the void.

"You will come with us," the Integration Unit said, his voice monotone and robotic. I glanced at him, then Perro. I thought of the Lieutenant as he'd been before the Hive got to him. Again. When I looked at him, I could think of little else.

Just a few days ago he'd been sitting across from Hunt, miserable, just like every new arrival to The Colony. He didn't deserve this. He'd fought in the war, survived capture, made it to the promised safety of The Colony—and the Hive had found him here just days later. He'd been a loyal warrior and I was angry for the Prillon he'd been, even more disgusted that this had happened to him here on the supposedly safe planet, right under our noses.

Hunt glanced at me, then went to stand beside the Hive unit. He didn't have to say anything. I felt it all. Rage, frustration, resolve, determination. We were either getting out of this whole—or as whole as we were now—or we would die. I'd somehow kill Hunt myself before letting him get strapped onto a fucking torture table. He'd do the same for me.

He walked down the long hallway, past a row of empty cells as I stepped in beside Perro. There had been nothing we could do from the containment cell. Now was the chance to find an escape, a way out of this. We needed to get free and get word to Base 3, to tell them where to find this underground hell and destroy it.

I felt the nudge of an ion pistol against my side, pressed up beneath the top half in the space where there was no armor. I didn't need a weapon jabbing me to force me to walk. I was already on my way to whatever fucked up shit they thought they were going to do to us. Perro pressed the gun again. I narrowed my eyes, looked down at the weapon, ready to tell him to fuck off. He might have been my ally once, but no longer.

But the gun wasn't pointed at me. No, Perro was pressing the hilt into my side. I raised my head in surprise, looked him in the eye, the one good eye he had left, and nearly stumbled. "Take it," he breathed. I barely heard him and my eyes widened. Neither of us faltered in our steps, knowing what he was doing might be witnessed. "But you must kill me."

You must kill me. Yes, he knew his fate, knew that the glimmer of the warrior that was left in his body was no competition for whatever the fuck they'd done to his brain. How had a sliver of him remained? But if he was in there, then he could be saved.

I took the weapon, settled it familiarly in my hand, my arm behind my back to keep it hidden from the Hive Unit in front of us.

"We will take you with us," I whispered. He was a good warrior, one of us. I would not leave him behind if there was a chance for him.

He shook his head once. "I'm lucid now, but I'm done. It's taking over, minute by minute. I'm fading, forgetting. There's almost nothing left. Kill me."

I saw his head jerk, his clear eye going blank. His hand gripped my arm painfully. His steps became rigid, just like the Hive unit in front of him. From one instant to the next, he was no longer Lieutenant Perro of the Coalition Fleet. There was nothing left of the Prillon warrior.

I wasn't sure if there was a glitch or if he wasn't finished with his transition, but he'd been there, if only for a few seconds. Would he return again? Could I save him during a lucid moment?

I had to test it, to see if he could be saved.

"Perro, don't let them do this," I said, my voice loud.

Hunt turned his head, looked at me, but I ignored him. He'd sensed the change in my emotions through the collar. While he might not know what had just transpired, he'd sense a hope that wasn't there just a minute ago. A new resolve to get our fellow warrior out, too. "You're a fucking Prillon, not a Hive."

Nothing. No response.

I tried again. "Warrior, armor up." I gave my best command voice, used the words that were always given by a commanding officer before going into battle.

Perro's head turned, met my gaze and I watched as his pupil dilated, his grip loosened but did not drop away. "Sir," he replied, but the Hive Unit beside Hunt stopped and turned. He pressed a button on the comm unit on his wrist and Lieutenant Perro's body convulsed. He didn't fall to the ground, but it was as if he'd been shocked, as if the Hive brain implant had been rebooted. When the Hive lifted his finger, Perro stilled. His hand fell, the eye black again. Empty. I knew then he was gone. For good? I couldn't be sure, but he'd been right. There was nothing left. He didn't deserve to be left this way. He deserved an honorable death, a warrior's death, instead of being controlled by a comm unit.

He'd given me the gun in one of his last moments of lucidity to save ourselves and perhaps some of the others. I would give him his final wish. I would set him free.

Seemingly satisfied—I had no idea how a Hive unit could have feelings—the Hive who'd reset Perro turned and began walking again.

My mind was processing everything so quickly it was hard to analyze. Perro had been cognizant enough to help, perhaps in his last moments as a Prillon, or he wanted to ensure I helped him escape. Perhaps he'd held on, fought the processing enough to get to us, to escape in the only way available to him. Death.

But now we were free, at least out from behind the energy field. Out here, my strength couldn't be contained. When I'd been captured by the Hive the first time, they'd made me powerful, strong. No, beyond strong. My bones, my muscles had been altered and I made an Atlan beast look like a small child. The Hive unit in front of me was no competition. I could rip the head from his body while maintaining mental clarity, unlike the beast. I could do it. I *would* do it. But I had to wait. Now was not the time to raise attention. We needed out of the brig and to see what was beyond. To see if there were others who needed rescuing as well. To discover if we faced a dozen Hive or a hundred.

All I knew was that we were still on The Colony, that there was this secret base, built and being used by the Hive to destroy the new life Hunt and I, and every warrior on The Colony, was building. It must be destroyed. The warriors would need a plan, or at the very least, information.

After I'd seen what I needed to see? Then all the technology the Hive had put in me would be used against them. They'd be destroyed by one of their own creations. They'd built a monster, and to get back to Kristin, I would unleash him.

The Hive were fucked.

14

K̶ristin, Outside Hive Secret Base

"How the hell did a secret Hive fortress get built on The Colony without anyone knowing?" I whispered. Kiel was beside me, both of us just peeking over the edge of a rock formation to see the entrance below. It was well fortified by rock, as if it had been built into a volcano or something. Guards manned the single wide door.

"I'm new to this planet," he said. "From what I understand, we arrived the same day."

The Everian was just as big as my mates, which was a surprise because they were downright huge. For someone of such large proportions, he was stealthy, his feet all but silent on the rocks as we'd followed the path he alone could see.

It was as if he had infrared vision or could see invisible bread crumbs or something, because he hadn't changed direction once since we'd left Krael's quarters. Part bloodhound? I had no idea, but the man was a fucking genius at tracking. No one else on the planet knew about this base—at least the good guys—and he brought us right here. Well, it hadn't been that easy. The trek had been long and there hadn't been an actual path to follow. No, I felt as if I'd climbed more rocks than a mountaineer scaling Everest. There wasn't a mountain—we hadn't gone up anything steep—but more over undulating formations that were sharp and craggy. My armor was scratched in several places from bumping the rocks and my hands were sore from gripping the rough surface to keep my balance.

But that was nothing. I knew beyond that entrance was an actual hell.

I looked to Kiel, the Hunter. I'd learned the *Hunter* was an actual title. Marz told me they were bounty hunters or police across the Coalition planets, depending on the occasion. Hunter was apt since he was so damned good at it. Everians were recruited by the Coalition, and assigned to elite assassination and recon units for just such a purpose. I hadn't asked, but I wondered if that was how he'd been caught by the Hive. I doubted I'd ever know, but apparently they hadn't done anything to weaken his abilities. Walking with him was strange, like walking with a psychic or something.

He knew where my mates were. He just seemed to *know*.

We were ahead of the others, scouts on this mission, as Rezzer and Marz watched our backs. Which was fine with me.

I saw no path, no sign of two huge Prillons, let alone a bunch of Hive.

"Since I wasn't here, I don't know how this place escaped their scans. There must be some kind of cloaking device."

He lifted his head, inspected the sheer rock faces around us. "Or magnetic interference from the rocks."

If I wasn't involved in this, I'd think he was talking sci-fi mumbo jumbo. But he had to be right. How else could this place avoid detection?

We remained still, watching as the guards were swapped out with replacements.

Hive.

I'd never seen them before. Ever.

But yeah, I'd watched a couple *Star Trek* movies. These things were like Captain Picard's borg, but bigger. Scarier. They weren't little humans turned into cyborgs, they were seven and eight-foot tall monsters coated in silver. They traveled in groups of three, always three. I'd heard about them, but Earth media had done a good job of downplaying their seriousness.

The Hive was a problem for other parts of the universe. Earth was safe. We were too strong, our defenses too great for them to invade.

Yeah, right. Earth had just been damn lucky the Coalition Fleet took us under their protection. So far. From what I knew of them now, no military force from any country on Earth would stand a chance against them.

Ever since we learned of the Hive, of other planets *out there,* I'd assumed they were just bad space aliens that had to be fought, like in the movies. Not...this. They didn't just kill, they consumed, destroyed lives. Ruined men. The Colony was proof of this.

Kiel, quiet beside me, was proof of this. I looked him over again, but still couldn't see where his scars were, if he had any, but it didn't matter. Everyone on this planet had survived hell. I didn't need to see silver on his skin to know he'd suffered. And yet here he was, leading me directly back to the enemy, to those who'd tortured him, who would have ultimately turned him into one of the Hive units standing guard.

These men were beyond brave.

"The other day, I came here from Earth, a bride," I said in a soft voice, sitting down on my butt, my back to the rock. "You came from being tortured by those things. Why would you want to risk your neck again? Especially when what was done to you is so fresh. I mean, aren't you scared?"

He studied me closely and I knew he was able to see more than most. As a Hunter, he could no doubt see things that weren't there for others. "Aren't you?" he asked me in return.

Kiel was the only one who hadn't argued when I said I was going to find my mates. Even the governor had balked at my help. But Kiel? I wasn't sure if he didn't care if I got myself killed or whether his hunting senses picked up that I wasn't just a female all in a tither about her lost mates. The way he looked at me now, I knew it was the latter. I'd been trained for this as he had, although I lacked his extra senses. Even without, I knew what I was doing. I'd lived, breathed, trained to track and save people. I had damn good instincts, and I was cool under pressure.

This mission was just as important as any other I'd ever been on. Bad guys liked to hurt people, kill them, spread destruction and ruin. Although, we'd never had the Hive where I came from. Didn't matter. Garbage was garbage no matter what planet I was on.

"This place so reminds me of a James Bond movie," I muttered, thinking Dr. No would be in his underground lair with all his minions trying to destroy the world. I was no

James Bond. With Kiel's good looks, he could fill the role, but he was just too big, too powerful. No one would look at the movie. Only him.

As for me, I had my mates somewhere behind that guarded door. While I admired Kiel, I adored my mates. And nothing was going to stop me from getting to them, not even a giant cyborg monster.

Kiel arched one brow at my movie comment, but said nothing.

"You are comfortable with your weapon?" he asked.

I pulled it from the holster, settled it into my grip. The cool metal was reassuring. Familiar. "Yes."

"Good." He knelt beside me. "While we only see one entrance, there is always another."

"Yeah, and where are his friends? You said they always travel in threes."

Kiel squinted over the rock, scanning the surroundings. "I believe they must be inside, just out of sight. But we will leave them be. The Hive would not have just one way to escape this place should there be an emergency or attack. We will find their second ingress and infiltrate from there."

Fancy Hunter, fancy words? Ingress? But then, maybe that was just my NPU trying to speak Everian. Whatever. I nodded, then followed as he sneaked back the way we'd come, Marz and Rezzer falling in behind us. Rachel had returned to Base 3 and I hoped she was rounding up the troops. Rezzer and Marz were leaving a trail, deep groves in the ground behind us every few feet so they could follow us. Hopefully, reinforcements would arrive soon.

As a group, we moved quietly. We were so far off Base 3, deep into the planet's cave and ravine system, that the standard communications weren't working. That left us a party of four. No backup. At least not now.

I wondered just how many Hive were inside that cave.

Kiel crept around a boulder and we fell in behind him in single file, Rezz on my six, which was cool. Nothing was getting past the beast.

The air smelled dry, like the Arizona desert in July. But it wasn't hot. I was comfortable in my armor, perhaps even a bit chilled with the faint light of the nearest star far from its zenith. I figured it was near dawn, or whatever they called it here. The light was weak and there was still the chill of night in the air.

It had been five hours since my mates had missed their check-in. Five hours which had sent the entire base into a frenzy. The news that warriors were going missing was a secret no longer. Governor Rone had everyone on lockdown, security doing room-to-room sweeps. But we knew the Hive weren't there, knew the bad guys weren't there. Krael was here, with my mates. I didn't have to be an Everian to know that.

If anyone could find my mates inside the labyrinth of caves that had to be under the surface of this planet, it was Kiel. That was why, with ion pistol raised and ready, I was following him into hell.

We had to find them. Not just my mates, but all the missing warriors. We had to shut this place down, destroy it so the threat would be over. So there would be peace on The Colony. The alternative was unthinkable.

Kristin, Secret Hive Base, The Colony

. . .

THE ROCK LEDGE where we lay sprawled on our bellies was no more than ten feet above the monsters. That's what the Hive were to me now, monsters. Just staring at them scared the shit out of me.

We were deep inside the planet's crust, the cavern we looked down upon was filled with activity. Two surgical stations were in the center, about thirty yards from our position, complete with lighting and a variety of computers and gadgets the likes of which I'd never seen. I did notice that nothing looked even remotely like anesthesia, which didn't shock me, but made me even angrier than before. I felt nauseated from what they were going to do to the warriors. What they had done. Was this what it had been like for Hunt and Tyran before they'd managed to escape? The others, too? The warriors flanking me? Knowing they'd been through this kind of torture and survived, only to be returned to Hive control now, would destroy even the strongest, the bravest among them.

The area appeared to be a natural rock formation, a vast cave, a place where drug dealers liked to use on Earth. Below, we saw three Hive and two prisoners. Those prisoners were my mates, who both appeared to be unharmed, at least so far. My heart leapt at the recognition, but it wasn't all happiness. I was close enough for my collar to sense them, to feel their emotions. They were hurt, I felt the edge of pain, but they hadn't been tortured. I felt hatred and determination.

I watched as Tyran lifted his head, his gaze swinging across the room. He'd sensed me, but didn't know where I was. My mind stilled, my own determination filling all of me. I couldn't allow them to sense my fear, my worry. Now wasn't the time. They needed to keep clear heads and if I was panicked, they would be, too.

Gripping my weapon, I looked to Kiel. Yes, I would take the others' strength, buoy myself so the men felt it and that alone. Perhaps my strength would work for them. They weren't free and they needed it for what was going to be done to them—

No. I wouldn't think about that. Focus. I narrowed my eyes and studied the enemy. As my mates had to pay attention to what was going on around them, I had to keep my head. The collars could be our downfall but I wouldn't let them. I studied the Hive in the cavern. Kiel had filled me in on the various types of units we might see as we'd been searching for the back entrance to their lair.

The Soldiers, like the one guarding the front entrance to this hell, and the one watching Hunt and Tyran a few feet to their left, were the biggest and strongest, supposedly the hardest to kill. They were integrated with enough technology to ensure that they were faster and stronger than any of the Coalition Fleet's warriors, except the Atlans in full beast mode. That Soldier stood between me and my mates, and I didn't like it.

Focus.

A Soldier classification was, I realized, the purpose the Hive had planned for my Tyran. When he'd been captured before, they'd been busy turning him into a Soldier, adding implants to his muscles and bones, making him Superman strong. Making him into the ultimate killer. But he'd gotten away.

But all the power was still inside his body, waiting to

explode from him. They'd created a formidable enemy, and he was mine.

The Hive who marched behind them with a large weapon pointed at Tyran's back was a Scout. With odd optical implants and an array of sensory material added to their flesh, the Scouts weren't meant for hand-to-hand combat. Kiel said they were still hard to kill, but were designed for striking hard and fast and running away. If Soldiers were their front line infantry, the Scouts were their snipers, pilots, or recon units. They were made to be quiet and quick.

And that's what they'd had in mind for Hunt.

But that was before, when my mates had been captured and tortured. I wondered what horrifying things they planned for my mates now. What else could there be? Tyran's strength didn't appear to matter. He was marching like a docile servant behind Hunt who followed the third Hive, this one a small, vicious Integration Unit, as the Scout brought up the rear.

The Scout that I recognized with a flash of horror. Next to me, Kiel stiffened as the Hive turned to scan the cavern and we both got out first clear look at his face. "Perro," he murmured.

The missing warrior. Shit. I hadn't met him before, but it wasn't him any longer.

But I didn't have time or energy to dwell on that. I returned my attention to the biggest threat in the room. The Integration Units, according to Kiel, were smart. While they followed orders, they could process various options and take the most ruthless action. And while the Soldiers followed orders and killed without mercy, they weren't cruel. They were little more than mindless killing machines manufactured by the thousands by the Hive central command.

But the Integration Units were sadistic, enjoyed torture, by programming or design, they enjoyed their work a little too much. And the way that little black-eyed bastard was watching my mates, he had plans to make them suffer.

Big plans.

Focus.

My eyes narrowed and I squeezed the ion blaster in my palm with impatience.

I was going to kill that one myself.

ristin

KIEL LEANED IN CLOSE, lifted his chin. "The Hive Unit with your mate, Tyran. That's Perro." His voice was no more than a whisper. "He's been integrated."

Shit. "So we shoot him?" I whispered back.

He nodded once, his lips tightening into a thin line. "We will not leave him here like this." Which meant he would kill him, put him out of his misery. "He will die a warrior's death."

I wanted to swear, stomp my feet, scream. Anything to let the anguish out. But no. I needed to keep my head. My mates, the others, needed me. I couldn't let my mates sense anything wrong, especially from me. Besides, they obviously were well aware of Perro's fate.

I nodded once, more determined than ever to finish this.

I was about to tell Kiel that I was ready when the hair on my arms rose and a shiver raced down my spine.

Instincts were king, and I blinked once, slowly, to clear my vision and my head before turning back to look down into the cavern again. I'd missed something. The chill racing over my skin was screaming at me to look again.

Beside me, Kiel's pointing finger uncurled and shifted a few degrees to the left, pointing. He sensed it, too. Looking in that direction, I trembled with adrenaline when I saw Krael leaning casually against the wall like he didn't have a care in the world. I'd only seen pictures of him, but I recognized him instantly. I had no doubt as to his identity. I'd spent hours and hours studying his military records, interviewing the people he knew and worked with on Base 3. I knew more about that asshole than his own mother.

He was dressed in Coalition body armor, like he was still part of the Fleet. He didn't look Hive. Being new to The Colony, Kiel hadn't met him either, but he'd seen the same pictures and the Coalition attire was a dead giveaway, especially since he didn't have an ion pistol pointed at him.

So what the hell was going on here besides the fact he thought he'd won?

In fact, that evil fucker was *grinning* at my mates, no doubt impatient for their torture to begin.

Over my dead body.

Focus, Webster.

I scooted back a few inches and Kiel followed. When we were face to face again, I didn't waste time and I didn't give him a chance to argue. My whisper was barely audible, but I knew, with his supposed advanced Hunter hearing, he'd have no trouble deciphering every word. "You get the

Integration Unit. Let Rezz and Marz take care of the other two. Krael is mine."

Kiel didn't argue, he smiled, and I decided right then and there that we were going to be friends. "How are you getting down there, Lady Zakar?"

"You're jumping, right?" There was enough ledge that we could run around to a point where it dipped close to the floor of the cavern, but that low point was halfway across the room. We'd never make it without being seen. At this location, we were between ten and fifteen feet off the ground. It was high, but I'd landed worse.

"Yes."

I peeked over the edge, saw that Tyran's gaze was scanning the room, looking for something. Me. Meanwhile, Hunt was allowing them to lead him toward the first operating table like a lamb to slaughter.

Fuck. That.

I turned to Kiel. We were out of time. "Ready?"

He nodded, the movement almost imperceptible. I nodded back, our gazes locking for a moment. I wasn't going home without my mates, and I needed him to understand that fact. "Go."

With that one word I rolled over the edge of the ledge and leapt to the ground as quietly as I could. The impact was jarring, but I knew what to expect, allowing my knees to bend so I didn't absorb all the impact, then rolled twice and came to my feet. Adrenaline pumped through me, so I wasn't even dizzy. I fired immediately at Krael.

He grunted as I hit him dead center in the chest, but the Prillon didn't go down. I hit him again in the thigh before he could move or process what was happening as Kiel was already across the room, leaping on the Integration Unit.

Behind me, Rezz's roar filled the cavern like the rumble of a helicopter, making my ears hurt and my bones rattle, but it startled the Scout escorting Hunt.

I fired on Krael again, heard a scuffle from the direction of Tyran and the Hive Soldier I knew he was most likely fighting. My mate had been wearing manacles of some sort, but I knew those wouldn't stop him. Not for long. He'd been biding his time. Smart.

Krael staggered back against the rock wall as I hit him again in the shoulder, but he still didn't go down.

Damn this Coalition armor!

He met my gaze for a moment before slipping into the darkness of the cavern beyond him, a small, nearly black abyss that made seeing impossible. The path was unknown, and he would have the advantage. While I wanted him dead, that hadn't been the goal of this mission. It was rescue and recover, and there were more enemies to deal with before we could pursue that rat.

Cursing, I turned to find Hunt locked in a struggle with the Hive escort, a huge Soldier unit. That was, until Rezz walked up behind the Hive, picked him up and literally tore his body in half, the sound making me gag as blood sprayed everyone within range, covering Hunt and the stark white and silver of the operating table next to them.

I was frozen in place, unable to move as I took in the change that had taken over Rezz's body. The Atlan had been big before, ridiculously big. Comic book big. But now he looked like a nine-foot tall, non-green version of the Incredible Hulk.

"Dead." That one word held a whole lot of satisfaction and the air left my body as my mind processed what had just happened and I imagined it happening on a battlefield over and over, hundreds and hundreds of times as hundreds and hundreds of beasts charged or attached together. I couldn't imagine anything more terrifying.

No wonder my mates were so protective.

The pounding of boots sounded behind me and I heard Captain Marz shout as I turned to see two more Hive Soldiers emerge from a tunnel. The opening had been hidden from view by our vantage point directly above it.

Shit. They were close and they'd sneaked up behind us.

I lifted my gun, backing away and firing as the first one clashed with Marz. The second was headed straight for me.

"Kristin!" My name was a roar, and I knew it came from Tyran, his rage and fear for me buckling my knees as it blasted me through the collar. We'd all tempered our emotions, until now. I sank to one knee, fighting to keep my weapon raised and pointing at the Hive sprinting toward me because of the strength of the feelings through the damn collar.

"Control yourself!" Hunt yelled at him, and the overwhelming barrage of pain and helplessness faded enough that I could move.

I shoved to my feet, pushing back. Fired at the Hive no more than three paces from me.

The Hive leapt through the air and I rolled to avoid the strike, the ground hard. He had to have been Prillon once upon a time, before they murdered him and made him something else.

But the strike never came. Hunt and the Soldier collided in mid-air over my body, the force of Hunt's strike driving them back. I stayed down—I knew when to stay out of the way and let others fight—as Rezz jumped over me to yank the Hive from Hunt's arms and tear him in half right in front of me.

Hunt turned to face me, chest rising and falling with his deep breaths, his features coated in blood, but he'd never looked more perfect. I loved him. I loved him, and I let it pour out of me like an explosion.

He was walking toward me when I heard more ion blaster fire coming from the other side of the cavern.

Tyran. Kiel. How could I have forgotten?

I turned and watched with growing horror as Tyran fired an ion blaster into the Scout who'd been walking a few paces behind him when they first entered the cavern. Tyran kept firing, but the Hive kept coming. Perro kept coming.

Shaking my head, I lifted my blaster to my knee, braced my arm there and fired, hoping to hit him from the side.

My aim was true, but he didn't even notice, like the shot I landed on his hip was no more than a bee sting.

"Worthless piece of shit," I muttered, scolding the only weapon I had at hand. Captain Marz finished off his Hive and was standing guard at the tunnel entrance where our surprise visitors had appeared. I looked around to see the beast, Rezz, moving toward Kiel.

And Hunt? Hunt was standing over me like an avenging angel. Protecting me. And as much as I loved him for it, I couldn't stay down. That wasn't my style.

I shoved the worthless ion blaster back into my thigh holster and stood up, moving toward Tyran and the Hive who now had its hands around my mate's neck.

Oh, no. Hell no.

I was ready to charge in, but Hunt grabbed me by the arms and pulled me back against his chest. "He's fine, mate. Trust me. Watch."

As if Tyran had just been waiting for Hunt's words, he lifted the Hive over his head and threw him nearly ten feet through the air, the Hive's body slamming into the rock wall with a loud crash. My mate stalked over, grabbed him by the head and squeezed his head into pulp between his palms. I turned away as the Hive's head literally popped, the top half of his skull gone, the bones that had once been his face crumpled like aluminum foil in Tyran's grip.

And *that* was disgusting. Nausea rose, but I'd won that battle dozens of times in the past and I ignored it, turning away as a shudder passed through me. Hunt pulled me to his chest and I let him, wrapping my arms around his waist as I watched Kiel back the Hive Integration Unit into a corner.

Kiel and the Hive were facing off, circling each other like boxers with Kiel caging him in. What the hell was the Hunter doing? "Kill him, Kiel!" I yelled.

"No. We need him alive."

Right. Krael got away. We needed at least one of them for questioning. From the corner of my vision Tyran appeared, walked straight up to the Hive and lifted him off his feet, pinning him to the wall like a bug.

"Don't kill him!" Kiel commanded. "I need him alive," he repeated.

Tyran growled but his gaze turned to focus on me and Hunt. He looked like the rest of us, covered in gore, rattled. Angry.

I held his gaze and I let him feel me through the collar. I wasn't scared. Well, I was shaken up a bit, but that was all. And next time I came to a gunfight, I was bringing a bigger fucking gun.

The Integration Unit squirmed, but Tyran ignored him

completely, the kicks and twists of the Hive's body not even making him flinch.

"How long can you hold him?" Kiel asked.

Tyran shrugged. "As long as it takes."

Captain Marz shouted and Hunt and I both turned to face him.

He nodded in the direction of the cave. "Governor's coming."

Rezz's deep rumble filled the cavern. "Too late. All dead."

"Not all of them," I said, and I turned back to find Kiel watching me. Our gazes locked and I knew we were both thinking the same thing. This creature, the monster Tyran held pinned to the wall, was going to talk. He had to.

Seconds later, Rachel's mates, Maxim and Ryston, charged into the cave with my new BFF a few feet behind. Surrounded by about twenty guards, of course. How she'd talked them into allowing her to come along, I had no idea.

The governor took everything in at a glance. "How many escaped?"

"One," I said. A sense of complete failure weighed me down for a few seconds, but Hunt's arm wrapped around my waist and I took a deep breath. "One. And it was Krael."

Maxim's gaze moved to Rezz, who stood at the entrance of the tunnel that the traitor had used to make his escape. "You got your beast under control, Warlord?"

"Yes."

I watched, amazed as the Atlan shrank before my eyes, his armor automatically shrinking to adjust to his normal size. He shook his shoulders as if shrugging off a heavy coat. "I'm fine. But the bastard went that way." He tilted his head toward the darkness. "We should pursue."

"Agreed." Maxim nodded to several of his men and they jogged over to the Atlan, the entire lot of them disappearing inside the dark tunnel seconds later, only their heavy footfall lingering.

"And Perro?" The governor asked.

"He's dead," Tyran said, his voice flat. He tipped his head to the side and the governor looked to where Perro's crumpled body lay near a small rock formation. He wasn't moving. "I gave him what he wanted."

Yes, he was dead, but he was at peace. The Hive controlled him no more.

"Are there more? Did you find the others?" Ryston asked.

Hunt answered. "There are at least a dozen Hive in these caves. We found the others, but it's too late for them."

"Understood." The big Prillon governor nodded to one of his men. "Shoot to kill. Bring me Krael alive."

"Yes, sir." A second set of four men peeled away from the main group, following Rezzer and the others down the dark tunnel.

Ryston moved with three more guards to assist Kiel and Tyran with the Hive warrior they still had trapped. Surrounded by so many warriors, the enemy stopped fighting.

"No! Get back!" Kiel shouted, but it was too late. The Hive's eyes turned a deep black and he went limp in Tyran's hold. My mate shook the creature, confusion evident in the wrinkled lines of his face as Kiel cursed and threw his weapon to the ground.

"Gods be damned! No!"

"What happened?" Tyran asked.

Kiel waved his hand in the air as if the answer were irrelevant now. "The Integration Units are different. If there is a statistical chance of escape, they will wait for the opportunity. If not, if they—or whoever the hell is controlling them—feel that capture is imminent, they are eliminated. Their brain basically melts inside their head."

"Self-destruct mode?" Rachel whispered with something that sounded suspiciously like awe. Even with her voice so soft, the Hunter heard her clear across the room. That warrior had some seriously bionic ears.

"Yes. Exactly. With just Tyran and I near, the Hive considered it a statistical possibility it could escape. Once Ryston and the others arrived..." His voice faded away with disgust. Once the others arrived, the odds changed, and not in the Hive's favor.

"My apologies," Ryston spoke, bowing slightly at the waist to the Hunter. "I did not know."

Tyran dropped the dead Hive unceremoniously to the ground and looked at Maxim. "We must take Perro with us, give him an honorable end." He turned, pointed to the dead warrior. "After that, nothing but cleanup here." His gaze drifted to me and held as he finished his statement, "But I have a disobedient mate to take care of."

Rachel whirled on her heel, her eyes meeting mine. She was making the *oh-boy-now-you're-going-to-get-it* face, but there was concern in her gaze as she looked me over. "Are you all right? Did you get hurt?"

I glanced down at my armor. I was covered in blood and guts, just like the rest of the team. And yes, I thought of us as a team now. Me, Kiel, Rez and Marz. They were mine, not the same way Tyran and Hunt were mine, but mine all the same.

I shrugged, unconcerned. "It's not my blood."

"Okay. Good." She stepped closer, but tilted her chin. "But I'm not going to hug you."

I laughed. "That's okay. I wouldn't touch me right now either."

Tyran stepped right around her and buried his hand in my hair, tugging so I had to look up at him. "I would."

With Hunt's arm locked around my waist, and the entire room watching, Tyran kissed me. Hard.

 ristin

THE GOVERNOR SAVED me from embarrassing myself, his order loud, and brooking no argument. "Hunt. Tyran. No one is touching anyone until you two have clearance to be on Base from Doctor Surnen. You spent the last few hours under Hive control. You're not going anywhere without an armed escort until the Doctor says you're clear."

Tyran ended the kiss to turn and scowl in Maxim's general direction. I still couldn't sense everything he was feeling, his iron control over his emotions sparing me the full impact of our connection through the collars. He'd all but knocked me off my knees once already. Hunt held back as well. I was running on adrenaline, using the rush to keep my feet under me. I knew the shock, the shaking, the nightmares would come later as my mind tried to process what I'd just seen. But this time, I'd have my mates to hold me. This time, I wouldn't be facing the long dark nights alone.

Hunt was the one to respond. "We're fine. Untouched."

Much to my surprise, Tyran disagreed. "You're not fine. Your head's a mess. You'll probably end up in the Pod."

Hunt grunted and I felt a glimmer of his pain through my collar. Yes, they were shielding me well. "And you? You haven't come out of this without injury. You've got at least three broken fingers and a few broken ribs."

"You're *all* going," Maxim insisted. "Ryston, Rachel, take four men and escort everyone back to medical." He looked from his mate to his second and I recognized the calm, controlled façade that Hunt often wore. And though he was intimidating, Maxim didn't scare me, which was never a good thing when I was thinking about running my mouth. Like now.

"Do you have a forensic team here?" I looked to Rachel, who raised her eyebrows in an *I-have-no-idea* look.

She turned to her mate, who looked to her with a question in his eyes. "Rachel?"

Rachel practically beamed, and then it hit me, she was the science geek. This was probably right up her alley. Her mate knew that and wanted her advice. He saw her as an equal, her skills valuable to him and The Colony. Let her join them in this mission once they were assured she would be safe. And for the first time since I'd met her, I was jealous. "I don't think so, but I'll have to ask Doctor Surnen."

Ryston walked up behind her and placed his hands on her shoulders, his touch affectionate. "What is a forensic team?"

"A group of investigators, a team that uses scientific methods to solve crimes, like fingerprinting, DNA tests..."

I picked up where Rachel left off. "Blood spatter analysis, trace chemical analysis, crime scene reconstruction..."

"We have never had the need on The Colony," Maxim stated. "We have such teams on Prillon Prime, as well as in the battlegroups, but we have never had problems with criminal activity here. Until now."

"You've never had mates here before either," Rachel insisted.

"Or Hive." That was me, making everyone far from happy with the observation.

The governor's gaze drifted from his mate's face to mine, and his expression hardened. "Are you familiar with these forensic teams and what they do?"

"Yes. I'm not a scientist. Rachel will have to do the lab analysis. But I could put together a team and get what we need." I'd seen enough crime scenes over the years to know what we should look for and where to start. I could collect samples like a pro and get them to Rachel or others for testing.

"I'll help." Rachel volunteered. "And so will Doctor Surnen."

The governor nodded. "It's settled." He turned to the corner, to where Kiel knelt over the dead Hive, looking for something. I had no idea what he was doing. "Hunter."

Kiel lifted his head and met the governor's gaze. "Yes?"

"You will assist Lady Zakar. I am officially placing you two in charge of this investigation."

Hunt's arm tightened on my waist, but Tyran actually growled. "No."

I gritted my teeth and turned to him. "Yes."

"It's too dangerous." His expression had gone cold,

distant, but I wasn't backing down, not on this. It was too important.

"I'm a criminal investigator. It's what I do. It's my specialty."

"No."

I raised a brow and crossed my arms, stepping free of Hunt's hold on my waist to stare down the giant man I loved. "I am who I am, Tyran. If you don't like it, I guess you can find yourself another mate."

I dropped that bomb, right in his lap and turned to follow Ryston and the others back to Base 3 where I could get this blood off me and find a nice warm bed. Alone. I was all out of energy for dealing with bullshit at the moment. Every ounce of fire and willpower I'd possessed had been focused on finding my mates. And we had. We'd saved them.

I'd saved them. With Kiel's help. Kiel and Marz and that giant beast Rezz. I'd dragged them along, and they'd come looking for their friend. I felt bad for them, because we'd found Lieutenant Perro, but he'd been lost. Transformed. Beyond saving and Tyran had given him the death he'd wanted. But at least now his friends knew what happened to him. They had closure. It was more than some people got.

I could deal with Kiel, work with him to figure this out. I actually liked their group, Kiel, Marz and Rezzer. They were my friends. Best of all, they'd respected me and my choice. Backed me in the fight. Done their jobs and let me do mine.

I refused to go back into the hothouse like a good little orchid.

I wasn't a freaking orchid.

My throat burned with unshed tears that I willed away from my eyes. I wouldn't cry. I wouldn't give in to the heartbreak of knowing my men didn't give a flying fuck about what I could do. I needed to be a valuable member of society, not a mate sitting on a damn pedestal. I wasn't going to be a sex toy and nothing else, no matter how mind-blowing the sex.

Hunt and Tyran followed behind me, but I ignored them, totally tuning them out. One of them, most likely Hunt, reached out from behind me to place a hand on my shoulder. I shrugged him off and increased my pace. I didn't want them touching me. Not right now. Not when they felt the way they did. Maybe not ever again. They might want to fuck me, but that seemed to be *all* they wanted.

The tears that leaked from my eyes every few steps? I couldn't stop them. Those were nothing. Must have gotten some dirt in my eyes.

Tyran, Two Hours Later, Medical Station

Doctor Surnen ran the ReGen wand over my hand and I used every ounce of control I possessed to hold still long enough for him to do his job. My armor was gone, replaced by plain blue tunic and pants. I wasn't in battle, but I was more anxious than I'd been in that Hive cave.

Kristin was shutting me out. Shutting us out. I couldn't feel anything from our collars but emptiness. Disappointment. Ice cold determination. Something was wrong. Kirstin was heat and fire, passion and joy. Not this dark void.

An hour ago, Hunt had emerged from the ReGen pod,

his head healed. He was the only one still in his armor. He'd nearly collapsed when we arrived and they'd put him straight into the pod.

Governor Maxim had insisted we all go straight to the medical station and I hadn't argued, needing to know that Kristin was well. I didn't care about my damn fingers or my ribs. I cared about her, that she was whole. That she didn't have one scratch on her after the battle.

Now that the danger was past, and Hunt was healed, I couldn't take my eyes from our mate.

I wanted to fuck Kristin, to sink into her, into the pleasure that could only be found in her body. To forget our ordeal, to forget that she'd been in danger. That we could have lost her. I wanted to finally claim her, to make the worry of her being taken from us, of her belonging to another, go away. I wanted all the stress of life just to disappear. Hell, I wanted everything and everyone to disappear so that Hunt and I could be alone with our mate.

Once we'd been healed, my fingers no longer broken, Hunt's head fully recovered, I assumed we'd get her between us. Yes, I wanted to fuck her, but I also wanted to punish her. Gods, she'd gone into danger and she needed to know that would not be allowed.

I'd have rather died in that cave than have my beautiful mate suffer or be hurt. Or worse. Gods only knew what the Hive did to females.

Kristin was sitting in a chair on the opposite side of the medical station, arguing with the medical officer who was trying to run a ReGen wand over her.

"I'm fine."

"Lady Zakar, I must insist."

She rolled her eyes and sat motionless as the man did

his job, the ReGen wand scanning through the cream colored pants and tunic she'd been given by the medical staff. We'd all been stripped, bathed, examined—all but Hunt. I wanted her in blue, my blue, but the tunic was better than the armor she'd been wearing, armor soaked in blood. Hive blood.

It could as easily have been hers.

The moment the wand indicated she was well, she pushed the medical officer away and hopped up out of the chair like she was in a big hurry to go somewhere. And she was. Away from me. From us.

She hurried into the outlying corridor, but there would be no escaping us. Hunt and I both had been cleared by the doctor, and we'd both been waiting for her. We were no more than two steps behind.

Once we walked through the door to our quarters, I couldn't hold my tongue for one more moment.

"I want to spank your ass until it's a fiery shade of red."

My voice was deep and dominant, but it lacked the usual conviction. I knew Kristin heard it because when she turned to face me, her eyes didn't tip down in submission, but instead met mine in continued concern. I felt her persistent anger laced with confusion.

"Because I went to save you?" she asked.

"Because you risked your life for mine."

"For ours," Hunt added. He tugged his armor off over his head, let it drop to the floor. I felt his exhaustion and it weighed on mine.

"We're supposed to protect each other," she countered, hands on her hips.

I slowly shook my head, gripped the hem of her shirt in my fingers. "No, *we're* supposed to protect *you*."

Once the garment was clear of her head, I tossed it aside. Yes, there was the perfect skin, the perfect breasts I loved. I stroked a line along her shoulder reverently.

"You almost died today, and we're going to fight about this?" She shivered at my gentle touch and I felt a blast of her arousal. "I'm more than just a fuck toy, you know. I can't stand to be locked in this room. I'll go crazy. I'm going to work with Kiel and head up the forensic team."

"I will not have you hurt!" I shouted.

"Life happens." She shrugged but I recognized the iron will I'd come to admire rising within her. Hunt stood behind me, silently waiting for me to work through my raging emotions. He was calm, and I used him as an anchor.

"Hunt?"

"Smother her and she'll choose another, someone strong enough to let her do what makes her happy."

Fuck. When he put it like that, I felt like an ass. She'd said as much in the cave, but I'd thought her to be bluffing. Perhaps not. I knew she was right, that Hunt was right, but I couldn't stop the instincts raging in me to protect her, shelter her, keep her safe.

"You want to be a part of this forensic team?" I could barely speak the words.

I felt the need in her, the desire to be included, helpful. "Yes. And if you'd stop and think for a minute, it does its job *after* something happens. Not before, not during. I'll be surrounded by warriors at all times. I'll be safe."

What she said made sense. "You will no longer charge into battle?"

She rubbed her hands over her arms as if she were chilled. "I don't like fighting. I don't want to do that again. I hope that finding that underground fortress will make sure the Hive are eliminated, permanently."

"Krael escaped," Hunt added. "Danger will continue to lurk."

"Then we will face it together." She reached out and placed a hand on my cheek. "But I don't need to be confronting Hive to be happy. I'm perfectly content sticking to analysis and clean up."

Hunt's brow went up. "So you will not battle the Hive again?"

Kristin pursed her lips. "I don't *want* to, but if they're threatening you, I will do what I need to do. It's my choice."

I sighed, recognizing the semantics in the wording. She wanted a choice. We'd blatantly shared our feelings over her going headlong into danger. She wanted to be the one to decide what she did, to take our wishes into account as she did so. She wanted us to trust her.

Leaning into her touch, I sighed. "I still want to spank you. But I'm too damn tired to even lift my hand and bring it down on your ass." I knelt down before her, worked her pants off her hips, and pushed them off, along with her boots. I lifted my eyes to meet hers. "We're going to sleep, then we'll talk more."

I sighed, felt the heavy weight of exhaustion press down on me.

Standing, I took her hand and led her to the bed. Out of the corner of my eye, I saw Hunt head into the bathing room, heard the shower tube come on.

I tugged back the covers and Kristin climbed in. I stripped off my clothes and let it all drop to the floor.

"Lay down."

She settled into the center of the bed as Hunt came into

the room, went around the far side of the bed and slid in beside her.

My cock hardened at the sight of her. Naked, her breasts thrusting up, her nipples hardening. She was not shy with us, never had been, and her legs parted slightly and I was able to see the dewy desire. She may be upset with us, but she still wanted us. Just like a few days before when I took her in the maintenance room.

I wanted to fuck her then and there, but it wasn't time. I walked to the bathing room and didn't linger in the tube, only quickly cleaning last bits of blood and grime from the ordeal. More than needing the bath, I took a moment to settle my mind, relinquishing thoughts of Lieutenant Perro and his sad demise. The fate of the others, too.

Returning to the room just a minute or two later, I sensed Kristin remained unhappy, but Hunt was soothing her with his gentle touch, sliding it up and down her side, over her hip, across her belly. He wasn't touching her anywhere sexual. Not now, but his cock was rock hard and she was squirming.

All the blood rushed to mine and it throbbed, my balls ached to sink deep. She needed a good fucking. We all needed the intimacy, to know we were alive and whole.

I slid in bed beside her, pressed close so she felt each of her mates. I leaned up on my elbow, my head resting in my hand. My palm settled on her belly.

"You won't run off and choose another mate as we sleep?"

"I only ran off to find *you*." She tried to squirm away, but our hands on her easily kept her between us. "Do you know what it was like, not knowing if you were all right?"

Her panic flared into me and there was only one way to

soothe her. To know we were whole and here with her. Not just as warriors, but as her mates. We would give her what she needed.

I ignored her words. "Submit, Kristin." Her eyes widened slightly, but she licked her lips at my dominant tone. I had enough energy to give her what she needed after all. "We're here. We're safe. You found us, now it's our turn to take care of you, to keep you safe."

She shifted against our palms and I didn't feel her anger through the collar now, only...acceptance. Yes, our reassuring presence was exactly what she needed. She wanted to be caught between us. Held. Secure in the knowledge that we were the ones in charge. That we were all safe.

"When we were taken, your world spun out of control, didn't it?" I asked.

She nodded.

"Your confidence was shaken, your protection gone. Your mates were gone."

Tears filled her eyes.

"You were so brave, mate," Hunt added.

She turned her head to look at him, tears sliding down her cheeks and onto the bed.

"You don't need to be brave any longer. We're here."

Yes, Hunt was right. She didn't have to take all the responsibility on her small shoulders any more.

"Feel us, mate." With a finger, I turned her cheek so her shiny eyes met mine. Held. "Feel our power. It's keeping you between us. Right where you want to be. Stop fighting. Yield," I insisted.

The tears came then in a hot wave. I turned her into me, put her head on my chest and let her cry.

I glanced at Hunt, who nodded, stroking her back as she let it all come out. Exhausted herself, her crying tapered to hiccups, then sniffles, before she fell asleep.

Only then did we relax, give over to our own exhaustion, content in knowing Kristin was right where she should be. Between us.

I awoke with a start, forgetting where I was. There was no comparison between the uncomfortable, unforgiving confines of the underground prison and this warm bed, but my mind hadn't caught up to my physical form. I breathed as quietly as I could, stilling my racing heart.

Kristin and Tyran were both still asleep beside me. I could search out the time, discover how long we'd rested, but it mattered not.

We'd all been exhausted, too weary to do what we all wanted.

Tyran had been right. We needed rest first, then we'd take care of the claiming.

I felt his intention clearly. Kristin had threatened to leave us, to choose another. Neither of us could accept that.

We'd been cowards, wanting to keep our mate locked away like delicate, breakable glass.

While I never expected to admit it, she'd been right. We couldn't hobble her spirit by forcing her to remain inside our quarters. We could tell her to not go into a fucking battle or a death defying rescue mission, but we had to let her live, make her own choices.

I could accept that. What I could not accept was losing her because we were afraid.

I wanted my palm on her ass, too. Tyran may be the Primary, the dominant mate, but I was just as upset with her about her lack of concern for her wellbeing. I wanted her just as safe as Tyran. I'd sensed her defiance earlier, but I'd underestimated the depth of Tyran's reaction. So had she.

I wiped my hand over my face, felt the silver flesh surrounding my eye and flexed my arm, knew I was thankful that was all the Hive had done to me, that I hadn't been destroyed like Perro or the others. I was whole. I had a mate. I could live. Have a family. And all because of the miracle sleeping beside me.

Kristin was safe, asleep between us.

Tyran had survived.

We were still a family. My cock thickened, lengthened at the sight of her bare body. The sheet Tyran had tugged over us had fallen to her waist, her breasts on display. Full mounds, the plump pink tips pointed to the ceiling. They were full and lush, ready to be taken in my mouth and I knew they'd harden to tight points against my tongue.

I wanted her with a new desperation and she whimpered, sensing my feelings through the collars, but not enough to awaken.

A talk and a sound fucking were in order, but I needed a

taste first. I'd longed for the flavor of her pussy, the scent of her arousal coating my face. I'd thought of it as we'd been held captive. Sliding the sheet lower, her pussy became exposed. One knee was bent, opening her up for me. She was bare there; no blonde hair shielded her. I couldn't miss the slick seam, her inner folds so swollen and eager for us that they peeked out. And her little clit, my mouth watered at the sight of that pink pearl.

Shifting on the bed, I settled between her legs. A palm on her inner thigh, I pushed her leg wide into the spot I'd just vacated, then settled down, my face just above her woman's flesh.

I breathed in, reveled in her feminine scent.

I could delay no longer. With my hand right at the seam of her leg, I put my thumb on her outer lip and spread her open, offering up all her pink treasure.

Lowering my head, I licked her from that tight rosette of her ass, up past her weeping entrance and to her clit, taking it into my mouth.

She shifted again, the feel of my mouth making her stir. I had to shift my own hips, my cock trapped beneath me, hard and uncomfortable.

She'd been wet when I parted her thighs, but now, she was dripping, my chin coated. I lapped it up, but she made more and more.

Writhing now, she bumped into Tyran, who woke up, pushing up onto his hand. He blinked a few times, took in what was going on beside him, then grinned.

I didn't lift my head, didn't stop sucking one swollen fold into my mouth and then nibbling on it before switching to the other.

"She can't come," Tyran said. His voice was as hard as

his cock, but he whispered. We both wanted to see how long she would remain asleep with my sweet assault on her pussy. He leaned down, grabbed something off the floor. His pants. Taking her hands, he took hold of her wrists, wrapped them up and tied them to the headboard. Her arms were over her head, her back arched.

We would release her if she panicked, but now she was ours.

Tyran was right, I might want to spend hours between her thighs, but she hadn't earned the right to come yet. It was our job to give it to her. It was our job also to deny her until her body rocketed into orgasm, prolonging her pleasure, making her release so much more intense.

I looked up her body, over her soft belly, full breasts, to watch as her pale skin flushed a pretty pink, watched as her head moved from side to side, her lips parting. She tugged at the restraints and cried out her pleasure.

I knew what she liked, felt it through the collar, so I continued.

Her body stiffened when she came awake, her eyes flying open as she glanced first at the ceiling, then at Tyran, then lifted her head to look down at me.

She tugged at her wrists, glanced up to see how she was pinned.

I licked her again, distracting her.

"Oh my god," she groaned, tugging at her wrists even as her emotions flooded me with lust. "Please, I need to come."

Neither of us said anything. I continued to lick her, suck her, lave her as she writhed and begged. Each time I felt she was close, I eased up on my actions.

I felt her skin become slick with sweat, knew I was pushing her hard. We'd always relented and given her the pleasure she desired. Not this time. And my cock ached for it. My balls were full, filled with the seed I'd pump into her, mark her. Claim her. Soon.

Tyran had his cock in hand and he slowly stroked it watching her, but not touching. I knew it wasn't easing his own need any, but he did it nonetheless.

"What's the matter, Kristin?"

Her back arched and tears of frustration formed in the corners of her eyes. She wasn't sad, she wasn't hurt. No, she was needy and it only made me crazed. We were paying for this just as much as she.

"You're not letting me come," she whimpered.

"No, we're not."

"Why?" she cried, tugging at her bonds.

"This feeling you have right now? It's what we felt when we saw you jump down from that ledge into the middle of that cavern. We felt helpless, out of control, powerless."

"I had to save you!"

"Others could have done it," Tyran countered.

"I had to do it. You're mine," she vowed fiercely.

"Yes, we belong to you. But you will feel our lack of control."

"Fuck you," she added and I felt a flare of anger through the collar, but also her desire. She didn't want Tyran to untie her. She didn't want me to stop tasting her sweet pussy. She wanted more.

Tyran shook his head as he stroked up his cock, swiped his thumb through the pre-cum that oozed from the tip. He lifted it to her mouth, pressed against her lower lip.

"Open," he said and he pushed his thumb into her mouth.

Instantly, she licked and sucked on it as if it were a cock.

I couldn't help but groan against her dripping folds.

He pulled his thumb free and she was eager for more, eager for a cock. But she would be denied, at our expense.

"We are your mates. Who do you belong to?"

I sucked on her clit, pushed her to the brink, then lifted my mouth off her entirely.

"You!"

"And who do I belong to?"

Her head turned to look at Tyran, but she said nothing.

"Feel the truth, mate. What does the collar make you feel about that answer?"

"You're mine." She groaned but lifted her head to look down her body at me. "You're mine, too."

Fuck yes, I was hers. Devoted. I'd do anything for her, even let her put herself in danger, it that's what made her happy. I knew Tyran felt the same.

"That's right," he continued. "We don't want you jumping into danger, but this job, the forensic team, will be safe. We know you need something that is yours. Making sure every new member of The Colony feels included, like they belong, is part of our job. This includes you."

It was hard to sense her satisfaction in our words, for she was too far gone in her arousal. Her need pushed ours, but we had to get through this.

"We were matched to you, Kristin Webster from Earth. We will not stop you or lock you in this room again. I love you. I love everything about you. You are a fierce warrior where protecting your mates is concerned." He circled one breast with his hand, slid it to her belly. "I hope you will be as protective a mother."

As Tyran spoke, I gently laved her pussy. While I wanted

her to come, she needed to be clear headed enough to hear Tyran's words, to understand what he was telling her.

"Do you accept our claim?" I asked, my breath fanning her swollen flesh.

"Now?" She pushed into me lifting her hips toward my eager mouth.

"Yes. Now," Tyran confirmed. "I'll force myself to let you work with the Hunter, but I won't be able to unless you're mine. Really mine."

I sensed what he wanted next and lifted my head, moving back on the bed to kneel between her ankles as he issues his next command. "Up on all fours."

With his hands, he helped Kristin roll over onto her knees, her upper body down on the bed, her arms stretched long and still bound above her head.

I slid back up between her legs, this time on my back so her pussy hovered right over my face. I took hold of her hips, pulled her down so she was riding my face.

As I held her, Tyran's hand came down, a hard spanking on her upturned ass.

She cried out, the mix of bliss from my mouth on her pussy, of my stiff tongue spearing into her, fucking her shallowly, combined with the hot sting of Tyran's palm.

His hand peppered across her ass, one side then the next, hitting a new spot each time. She loved it. I felt it in the way her body stiffened after each resounding crack of palm against soft flesh, but when she instantly yielded after. The way her body kept her so wet and ready for our cocks.

"Please!" she wailed.

Tyran spanked her again, this time harder. "Who do you belong to, Kristin from Earth?"

Tyran's full dominance had returned. He'd recovered

from the injuries, refreshed from sleep and was ready to tend to our mate. To make her ours.

Completely.

He spanked her again. I continued to lick and lave.

I heard the container of lube open, heard the wet sound as Tyran spread it on his cock. I knew what he was going to do, felt his urgency as he prepared himself.

I finally slid out from beneath her, wiped her juices from my mouth. Tyran put his thumb against her back hole, coated it in lube, collected more from the container, then added more to her, readying her for his cock.

She pushed her hips back and his thumb slid in easily. She groaned and so did I. I felt her pleasure as strongly as if it were my own. I could deny my own cock no longer, gripping it and squeezing it, trying to delay my orgasm. I wanted to be deep inside her when I came, but I would only do that when we claimed her.

"Who do you belong to?" Tyran repeated. Seeing him fuck her ass with his thumb, the digit thickly coated in lube, sliding in deeper and deeper around parted cheeks that were a bright pink from her spanking.

I felt her fight, felt her need, felt everything blasting at us. But then, as if she'd been holding on to a ledge with the tips of her fingers, she let go. Every line of her body softened, she even whimpered in relief.

"You," she breathed.

Gods, she was gorgeous.

"Why?" I asked.

"Because you'll keep me safe, *know* what I need and give it to me."

"What else?"

"Let me be me, in bed and out."

"That's right, mate. You'll go about your day knowing your mates are here for you. Waiting. Ready to kill for you, die for you. All because we love you."

"We only spank *you*. We only fuck *you*. We only fill *your* ass," Tyran said as he continued to stretch her. He held my gaze and nodded toward my hand. I knew what he wanted. He wanted me to fill her pussy as he stretched her ass. It was time to make her scream with pleasure. "Because you're ours and we know *you enjoy it.*"

I moved forward and reached under her to slowly slide two fingers deep into her wet core as she collapsed with a sob.

"I love you, Kristin" he repeated. "You're mine."

She came then, a soft rolling orgasm, a long plaintive moan accompanying it. It wasn't like when we fucked her. No, that would come. This was a different kind of release, her body and mind giving over to us, succumbing and relenting. Loving it, us. Our dominance. Our acceptance of her as a strong and independent female.

Tyran stilled his thumb, let her savor the moment, for we felt it too. She was giving to us and we were giving to her.

When she caught her breath, she opened her eyes. Tyran leaned forward so he could look into her passion filled gaze. I saw the pale depths were filled with love. *Felt* it. If I were an Atlan beast, I'd beat my chest and roar.

"Claim me," her voice was breathless, but the words were an order, no less.

I stilled, slipping my fingers free. Those were the words I'd longed to hear since she arrived on the transport pad. Tyran grinned as he slipped his thumb from her. "You are aware the Prillon custom of claiming involves an audience.

Witnesses to the official act of us fucking your ass and pussy, filling you with our seed.

Her eyes widened, even with her cheek pressed into the bed. "No."

"You don't want us to claim you?" Tyran asked.

"Claim me, fuck me, but do it here. No audience. I don't need a witness. I know you're mine." She turned her head so that her forehead was pressed into the mattress, waiting. "You're both mine."

He nodded once and glanced at me. This was another breach in protocol, but we were beyond caring about customs or rules. We only cared about her.

"God, you two are making me crazy. Do it. Claim me. As long as it's right now."

I reached up, undid the knot from the headboard, then loosened the portion about her wrists, freeing her. Helping her up so she was kneeling, I rubbed her arms and shoulders, easing the muscles. Tyran settled onto his back on the bed, waiting. I helped her climb over his lap, but he turned her around, facing away from him.

"I love seeing my handprints on your ass," Tyran said, taking a hold of her hips and positioning her as he wanted, his cock nestled directly behind her.

"While we will not have witnesses," he said. "But we will say the words. Do you accept our claim, mate? Do you give yourself to me and my second freely, or do you wish to choose another primary mate?"

Kristin looked over her shoulder at Tyran, smiled at him. I felt a blast of love from the two of them.

"I accept your claim, warrior." She said it to Tyran, then turned back and looked at me. "I accept your claim, too," she repeated.

"Then we claim you in the rite of naming," I said, finishing the honored words spoken by Prillon mates for centuries. "You are mine and I shall kill any other warrior who dares to touch you."

"As will I," Tyran concluded.

"It's time," I told her. "Take his cock in your ass, mate. Tyran will help you. Once he's deep inside, I'll fill your pussy."

She nodded once and lifted up, then, with Tyran's hands on her for guidance, lowered her so his cock pressed against her ass. With Tyran having prepared the opening and the liberal application of lube, once Kristin took a deep breath and relaxed, she flowered open and his cock head slipped inside.

She groaned, then panted out her breaths as Tyran held her in place, keeping gravity from forcing her to be filled too quickly.

Reaching out, I brushed my thumb over a nipple, felt the softness of it as I watched it tighten. "You're taking him beautifully, mate. Just know, my balls are aching just from watching his cock disappear inside you."

She licked her lips and nodded once and Tyran knew to lower her down. Slowly, up and down he moved her, fucking her until he was in all the way and she was sitting on his lap.

I stroked my cock just from the thought of him buried within her.

"Ready for me, mate?"

Kristin puffed out a breath and gave me a shaky grin. I could see her clit protruding out and I licked my lips, the taste of her still on my tongue. "Yes, I want you in me, too."

"Lean back," I said and she placed her hands behind her on Tyran's torso. The angle exposed her pussy to me.

Tyran widened his legs and I moved between, gripping my cock and guiding it to her entrance. She was just as wet and her juices coated my crown. I met her pale eyes, saw her arousal, felt her readiness for this.

Shifting, I slid in, but she was so fucking tight. There was almost no room for me, with Tyran's cock pressing against mine through the thin membrane that separated us.

I held my breath as I worked my way in. I put one hand on the bed and leaned forward, our chests touching as I held her gaze and thrust deep.

"Yes!" she cried.

I groaned and Tyran's hips thrust up of their own volition.

"We're one, mate. It's time to claim you."

"Yes," she repeated, then again and again, making it a mantra as we began to fuck her, alternating strokes and then, once we could no longer resist our basest needs, began to fill her with deliberate abandon.

She clenched me like a fist. A hot, wet, perfect fist. I wasn't strong enough to last. I'd wanted this, dreamed of this moment while captured. I felt how much Kristin loved it through the collar, knew she was on the brink.

Tyran did, too, for he called out. "Come, mate. Come and we'll follow, marking you with our seed."

She arched her back and stilled, her eyes closed, her mouth open and she gave a throaty moan. I felt it in my bones, my heart, my balls. I couldn't hold back, especially the way her pussy was rippling and squeezing me even further. My balls tightened, emptied of seed and it spurted into her in thick, hot pulses. Her pleasure ratcheted up mine. Mine pushed Tyran over and he came deep inside her ass.

"Ours," Tyran called as he gripped her hips and filled her.

"Ours," I repeated as I knew we'd found the one perfect mate in all the universe. I watched as the collar about her neck changed from black to the Zakar blue. The claiming was complete. Yes, she was ours. Forever.

"Yours," Kristin panted, perfectly placed between us.

Where she belonged.

EPILOGUE

ristin

"ALL DONE?" Rachel asked, coming into the room designated as the new forensic lab. It was down the hall from Rachel's space in the medical section of Base 3. Kiel and a few others worked with me daily to study evidence collected from the underground fortress. Almost every day, we returned there and mapped the labyrinth of tunnels. We found more evidence of the Hive every trip. Worse, we knew they weren't gone. We hadn't won. They'd just moved on. Every Base on The Colony had been alerted to the problem and Prime Nial had designated additional battleships to patrol the space between The Colony and Hive controlled space.

Everyone's goal was to find Krael, to bring him to justice before he devised any new evil plans.

It had been a full month since I'd arrived, since the

warriors went missing. Three weeks since my claiming. My hand drifted to the collar, now blue to match my clothing and my mates' collars. Once upon a time, I'd thought to tease Tyran by wearing orange or red or black. Any other color.

But the buzz of contentment he sent my way every time he or Hunt saw me wearing Zakar family colors killed the urge. Their happiness was my favorite drug.

While Tyran and Hunt weren't thrilled with me being anywhere but at their sides, they recognized after they'd been rescued that stifling me wasn't going to make me happy. Tyran had been right, the match meant I had to be myself, which was an independent woman. If they'd wanted a doormat, the Interstellar Brides Program would have given them one.

I nodded, turned off the light at my workstation. Rachel hooked arms with me and led me down the hall. "Good, our mates are waiting for us."

We were to meet them in the communal dining area. I was eager to see them, to tell them my news. I'd sworn Doctor Surnen to secrecy, but he was practically glowing, so I knew he wouldn't last long.

There hadn't been a baby on The Colony, well, ever.

"Do they know?" she asked.

I nodded to an Atlan we passed, then glanced at Rachel. "I don't know how they can't. The dang collars don't allow any secrets."

"A woman should tell her men she's having their baby on her own time, not because they're damn mind readers."

I'd thrown up in the lab the day before and Rachel had been the one to make me consider the possibility that I wasn't sick, but pregnant. As soon as the thought entered my head, I knew it to be true.

I was hornier than ever—not that I'd told her that—and my breasts were tender. Sensitive. My mates still liked to tie me up and have their way with me. I loved it—of course they knew that, too—but they were proud of me for using my abilities to help The Colony. Just as Rachel had. And that acceptance was the last thing I'd needed. Everything inside me clicked into place and I'd never been happier, more content. I was so happy that I'd started waiting for the other shoe to drop.

No one could be this happy. It didn't seem possible. I was still half afraid that this was all just a dream and I was going to wake up.

Things were too perfect. I could be assertive at work and submissive behind closed doors. I just had to wonder once they found out about the baby if they'd treat me differently. I didn't want them to stop dominating me in bed. Their alpha attitudes made me so hot I lost my mind. I was half afraid they wouldn't spank me, or fuck me, for fear of hurting me or our unborn child. I'd heard of men like that on Earth. Once their woman was pregnant, it freaked them out. Turned them off.

I'd die. I'd come to count on the heat constantly blazing from my mates' eyes.

We entered the dining room. A number of warriors were in groups, eating and chatting. But my eyes were drawn only to my mates. They stood, along with Maxim and Ryston, at our arrival. While they nodded at Rachel, my mates only had eyes for me as well.

"Have something you want to tell us?" Hunt asked.

I looked to Rachel, who was being pulled into Ryston's arms as Maxim kissed the top of her head.

"Mind readers." She laughed, rolled her eyes, then gave her attention to her mates.

Hunt took me by the arm, led me out of the room and down the hall. "Where are we going? I thought we were having dinner with the others."

Tyran scooped me up into his arms, held me close. "I think there's something you want to tell us. Something small, but getting bigger by the minute."

I saw the heat in his gaze, the love, felt both blast me through the collar. I was glad he held me, for Hunt's emotional assault was powerful.

"Oh," I gasped, tugged at the collar. "You already know?" A shadow of disappointment hovered. I'd wanted to surprise them. I really, really did.

"Say it," Tyran said.

I looked to him, then glanced at Hunt, who stood in front of us, his gaze blazing with just as much love and heat. I was sheltered between them.

"We're having a baby."

Hunt whooped for joy, surprising warriors who passed.

I couldn't help the smile that spread across my face. "This doesn't mean I won't be working, or that you'll be carrying me like this everywhere for the next nine months," I grumbled.

Tyran carried me in the direction of our quarters with Hunt walking alongside. "We will not hold you back, mate. But you must not take risks."

Hunt scowled. "I will discuss this with Kiel. We will double her guard."

Tyran nodded. "Good. I will speak with the governor and cut back her hours."

"You'll do no such thing!" I smacked Tyran on the shoulder and Hunt on the chest, stretching to reach him. "Women work and have babies all the time." When they both grinned, the joke was up. "You two are terrible."

I'd fought long and hard for my independence. I probably would rest more as I got bigger. I had no idea just how big a Prillon baby might be, but based on my mates, I was guessing a healthy ten pound bundle of joy wasn't an unlikely outcome.

Hunt reached over and brushed his finger along my cheek. "You know we just want you to be safe."

"I know. I'm careful."

"You better be." Tyran practically growled, but I felt the swirl of contentment between all three of us. This was what I'd wanted when I walked into the testing center all those months ago. Men who loved me, protected me, respected me. Made me whole, just as I did for them. And a baby? That was my bonus prize.

"But I don't want you to be too careful," I insisted, and let my hardcore lust for my mates blast them through the collars. Tyran's step faltered, but he recovered quickly.

"Don't worry. This doesn't mean we won't tie you to the bed and have our way with you."

My sensitive nipples hardened. They knew how much I liked that, submitting and giving myself to them, just as they gave every part of themselves to me in return.

"Yes, please," I replied.

A SPECIAL THANK YOU TO MY READERS...

Want more? I've got *hidden* bonus content on my web site *exclusively* for those on my <u>mailing list.</u>

If you are already on my email list, you don't need to do a thing! Simply scroll to the bottom of my newsletter emails and click on the *super-secret* link.

Not a member? What are you waiting for? In addition to ALL of my bonus content (great new stuff will be added regularly) you will be the first to hear about my newest release the second it hits the stores—AND you will get a free book as a special welcome gift.

Sign up now! http://freescifiromance.com

FIND YOUR INTERSTELLAR MATCH!

YOUR mate is out there. Take the test today and discover your perfect match. Are you ready for a sexy alien mate (or two)?

VOLUNTEER NOW!

interstellarbridesprogram.com

DO YOU LOVE AUDIOBOOKS?

Grace Goodwin's books are now available as
audiobooks...everywhere.

LET'S TALK SPOILER ROOM!

Interested in joining my **Sci-Fi Squad**? Meet new like-minded sci-fi romance fanatics and chat with Grace! Get excerpts, cover reveals and sneak peeks before anyone else. Be part of a private Facebook group that shares pictures and fun news! Join here:

https://www.facebook.com/groups/scifisquad/

***

Want to talk about Grace Goodwin books with others? Join the **SPOILER ROOM** and spoil away! Your GG BFFs are waiting! (And so is Grace)

Join here:

https://www.facebook.com/groups/ggspoilerroom/

GET A FREE BOOK!

Join my mailing list to be the first to know of new releases, free books, special prices and other author giveaways.

http://freescifiromance.com

ALSO BY GRACE GOODWIN

Cyborg Seduction

Her Cyborg Beast

Cyborg Fever

Rogue Cyborg

Cyborg's Secret Baby

Interstellar Brides® Program: The Virgins

The Alien's Mate

Claiming His Virgin

His Virgin Mate

His Virgin Bride

Interstellar Brides® Program: Ascension Saga

Ascension Saga, book 1

Ascension Saga, book 2

Ascension Saga, book 3

Trinity: Ascension Saga - Volume 1

Ascension Saga, book 4

Ascension Saga, book 5

Ascension Saga, book 6

Faith: Ascension Saga - Volume 2

Ascension Saga, book 7

Ascension Saga, book 8

Ascension Saga, book 9

Destiny: Ascension Saga - Volume 3

Other Books

Their Conquered Bride

Wild Wolf Claiming: A Howl's Romance

ABOUT GRACE

Grace Goodwin is a *USA Today* and international bestselling author of Sci-Fi & Paranormal romance. Grace believes all women should be treated like royalty, in the bedroom and out of it, and writes love stories where men know how to make their women feel pampered, protected and very well taken care of. Grace hates the snow, loves the mountains (yes, that's a problem) and wishes she could simply download the stories out of her head instead of being forced to type them out. Grace lives in the western US and is a full-time writer, an avid reader and an admitted caffeine addict. She is active on Facebook and loves to chat with readers and fellow sci-fi fanatics.

All of Grace's books can be read as sexy, stand-alone adventures. But be careful, she likes her heroes hot and her love scenes hotter. You have been warned...

www.gracegoodwin.com
gracegoodwinauthor@gmail.com